MICHAEL RYMER entered the University of Southern California in 1981 to study film. Whilst at USC he made several short films for which he was awarded the Warner Communication Scholarship for Directing. He was selected to direct one of the advanced senior projects, *The Cut*, a documentary about a hairdressing salon which attracted critical praise.

In 1986 Rymer enrolled in an intensive two-year Stanislavsky-based training program for actors. During this time he wrote and directed two plays: *Darkness At Noon* and *Ensenada*, staged at the Los Angeles Art Theatre.

In 1989 Rymer wrote *Dead Sleep* a psychological thriller which was bought by Village Roadshow and produced at their Queensland studios in 1990. Other commissions followed, including *Never Surrender* (for Village Roadshow), *Mommy's Little Monster* (for Shadowhill Entertainment) and *Electric Dreaming*, a contemporary romantic comedy set in the Australian outback. Most recently Rymer was commissioned by Warner Bros to rewrite *The Flood* for NBC, filmed on location in Queensland. *Angel Baby* marked his feature-film directorial debut.

Angel Baby

Original Screenplay by
Michael Rymer

Currency Press • Sydney

First published 1996 by
Currency Press Ltd,
PO Box 452, Paddington,
NSW 2021, Australia

10 9 8 7 6 5 4 3 2 1 0

NATIONAL LIBRARY OF AUSTRALIA CIP DATA
Rymer, Michael, 1963
   Angel baby : original screenplay.
   ISBN 0 86819 457 3.
   I. Title. II. Title: Angel baby (Motion picture : 1995).
791.4372

Printed by Southwood Press, Marrickville, NSW.
Cover design by Trevor Hood/Anaconda Design

PHOTOGRAPHIC ACKNOWLEDGMENTS: All production stills used on the cover and appearing within the text were taken by Jennifer Mitchell.

Front cover: Jacqueline McKenzie as Kate and John Lynch as Harry; p.ii, Kate and Harry; p.vi Kate; p.xxii Kate and Harry; p.2 Harry; p.16 Harry and Kate; p.33 Kate; p.38 Harry and Kate; p.44 Kate and Harry; Deborra-lee Furness as Louise Goodman, Kate and Harry; p.75 (above) Harry and Kate; p.75 (below) David Argue as Dave, Geoff Brooks as Rowen, Humphrey Bower as Frank and Harry; p.82 Harry, Colin Friels as Morris Goodman and Daniel Daperis as Sam Goodman; p.90 Harry and Morris.

Contents

Presiding Over Accidents

Michael Rymer

People said 'You should keep a diary.' I'm not sure whether it was a fear of hubris or just plain laziness that caused me not to do it. My best record of the genesis of *Angel Baby* is in the path that the innumerable drafts took, going back to the initial notes and character sketches. Reading these has triggered specific memories of turning points in the creative process.

WRITING
Angel Baby was conceived in our Hollywood Hills house in autumn 1990. I spent many an early morning out in the garage which the previous owner had converted into an office. He had ripped out the back wall, so the carpet was constantly damp and the sliding glass door did not sit flush to the wall. And yet it was the perfect writing environment. I would sit at my Mac, my Prussian Blue cat on my lap (also named Mac), a small heater at my feet. Half of the battle of writing is actually doing it, accompanied in my case by big mugs of tea, music, and a small library of books to dip into every time I needed stimulus or a distraction.

I had been working as a screenwriter for a couple of years, but I was still struggling. The original plan was to become a successful writer and parlay that into a directing career. As I went broke that summer trying to keep up the mortgage payments, I began to realize that this was not the best way to approach things. So I changed direction. I had enough unpleasant experiences as a writer. Decent work ruined by a bad director, or just gathering dust on a producer's shelf. So the first inspiration was a practical one – I was going to write a screenplay that I could direct.

In the years leading up to *Angel Baby*, I had taught myself to write by cranking out screenplay after screenplay. At first I would write very elaborate visual scenes, but I began to realize that these were very hard for the reader to understand. I became frustrated because I knew exactly how I would cross cut two sequences, or use a piece of music in counter-point. Things impossible to describe in words. I'd say 'Look at any Peter Weir film. Who would have known that a ten minute sequence in which the Amish build a barn would have so much meaning.' But that wasn't much help, because I wasn't Peter Weir.

So I developed a writing style that was much more 'literary'. More emphasis on dialogue. Less description. The main thing about the screenplay was that it became 'a good read.' A good example of this in *Angel Baby* is the bowling scene – originally that had very specific dialogue which I thought was funny and good character establishment. When we shot it, we shot the dialogue and also a lot of other improvised material. But the sequence became part of the opening titles sequence with loud rock music. The specific lines became irrelevant. We ended up cutting it purely for image.

One nice thing I've noticed about watching the film with subtitles is that every little line, every ad lib, every aside, is printed in bold letters, so the audience gets a whole layer of the film that most English speaking audiences don't get on first viewing.

In film school, we had a purist aesthetic about the importance of visual communication. We would poo-poo films that relied on dialogue and praise films that used 'filmic' techniques to convey ideas. (This was before the Tarantino era.) Subsequently, I found that the films that excited me were actually very dependent on dialogue and character: *Good Fellas* and *Drugstore Cowboy* were two seminal films for me, and I began to see brilliant low budget work which achieved enormous effect with people basically talking in rooms, particularly *Withnail & I, Prick Up Your Ears, After Dark My Sweet, Sid and Nancy* and *Sex, Lies and Videotape*. These films depended on good writing and acting, and that became my priority.

I knew the subject matter would have to be a love story. It would be fairly dark and intense because that's my taste. I was and am very much in love with my wife, Loretta, and in those days I had a strong ambivalence about physical violence. Loretta is some nineteen years older than I am, and many of our friends had warned us that our relationship could not possibly last. It was exactly this sort of opposition that caused us to stick together even more and rise above the petty squabbles that might have weakened our relationship. I don't know how conscious a decision it was, but *Angel Baby* certainly reflects my feelings about my marriage – that true love can give a higher purpose, to transcend the ordinary, and bring out the best qualities in the individual such as courage, commitment, passion and faith.

I had read that good filmmaking was 'the art of conveying the filmmaker's fascination with a subject to the audience.' My personal preoccupation was the occult. I had a large collection of Tarot cards, books on Kabalah, Geomancy, Tantric Yoga, Eastern Spiritualism, as well as many books on mythology and anthropology. I poured all this into *Angel Baby* but continually removed any direct references. This story would have a strong mythological basis, but only where it counted – on an unconscious level. The idea of creating the special circumstances to bring down a 'special soul' or an angel child was fairly common in occult literature. And the story of two outcasts, on the run, giving birth to a Messiah, predates the book of Exodus by who knows how long.

The first scene I wrote was after Harry and Kate make love, when Harry wakes up to find himself tied up. I didn't know why he was tied up, I didn't know what it meant, but I liked the characters and so I built backwards from there. I had about eighty pages of material before it occurred to me that most people would consider these characters, with their superstitions, delusions, rituals and heightened sense of reality as 'crazy'. I went and bought a couple of books on mental illness.

My first thought was to use the notion that mentally ill people were visionaries, mavericks who could 'see' the world more clearly and so did not fit in to our limited timid structures. This was a notion very much derived from *One Flew Over The Cuckoo's Nest*, reinforced by a couple of books by R.D. Lang. I had also written a film about the Chelmsford Scandal in which a doctor had misused his power to drug and abuse patients. So I was predisposed to judge the medical community and drug companies very harshly. Within the psychiatric community, there's always a lot of debate. Talking therapy versus Medication, Environmental causes verses Genetic. It is easy to research the subject of mental illness because there are many organisations and support groups very willing to talk and share their experiences. For years, mental illness was a shameful thing, locked in the closet, never spoken about. This was fuelled by the idea that mental illness is caused by some childhood trauma, and therefore the parents are to blame. I can't think of a single idea that has caused more pain and suffering than that one misconception to already traumatised parents. Later, when my research expanded into the Australian scene, I even discovered I had a couple of relatives of my own in institutions.

After talking to enough people, I began to realise that *Cuckoo's Nest* was more a story about the sixties, about the individual versus institutions. That medication was not a bad thing – that it helped many people function and lead relatively normal lives. This was particularly true in the nineties, as the types of medication became more sophisticated and subtle.

So, I had to abandon my simple idea that Harry and Kate were visionaries, but in return I gained a very powerful story element – if Harry and Kate went off their medication, as many clients do, they would have to do battle with psychotic episodes. What more omnipotent and terrifying villain could there be, than the demons of one's own unconscious mind! Originally, Kate was in a very destructive and dangerous relationship with a powerful and manipulative older man. I quickly got rid of this character although he hung around for many more drafts in a younger knife-wielding form, in order to trigger Kate's breakdowns.

I spent several months meeting parents, talking to doctors and clients. Then I settled into a routine of going to the Glendale Club House every morning from nine until lunch. It took about a week before the people there would start opening up to me. They would show me their note books, filled with wild drawings and diagrams. Raves about God, the Devil, Jesus, UFOs, government conspiracies etc. I played pool, I listened to their movie ideas, I went bowling with them. I remember that it was during the Gulf War, and everyone else in Los Angeles was anxious and upset, riveted to the television, waiting for Saddam's 'Mother of All Battles'. I asked the clients what they thought of the war and most of them had no idea that it was going on. The atmosphere at the Clubhouse was a feeling of peace and absolutely no pressure – I actually began to look forward to going there because it was a place where I had no responsibilities, no obligation to 'achieve'. On occasions there would be a flurry of psychosis which would spread through the room like a wave. A client would have gone off their medication and their behaviour would trigger an electric disturbance throughout the room. I would leave with my head fried. And it was then that I realised how difficult it would be for anyone there to become functional – how important would their need be for 'normality'.

Usually I find that the period of research is over when I can't be bothered doing any more. It's not a decision as much as a throwing up of the hands. Enough! Get on with it! There was a point where I had gathered enough scenes and material together to start structuring a story. And then it began to have a momentum of its own. I found myself writing sequences as if they were being channelled through me. It was the easy part. The mystic in me believes very much in the collective unconscious and tapping into a higher source. But I think it was a function of patience and waiting for the story to form properly before launching in – because the basic elements of the story were strong.

The idea was to write the script and make the film any way I could: with a Super 8 camera if I had to, on weekends, on a credit card, the usual guerrilla approach. Usually, once there's a solid draft, I invite some actors around to read the script in real time. It gives me an indication of the temporal sense of the story telling. I'll also invite a few 'listeners' – friends in the industry whose opinions I respect. In the case of *Angel Baby*, the reaction was immediate and strong and I had people in the room wanting to produce the script immediately. Sounded good to me.

FINANCING
The story of the film's financing is too sordid to go into detail. I will say there were several offers to sell the script if I would agree not to direct it. People cajoled, taunted and threatened me. They sneered 'What makes you think you can do this?' But it wasn't

until one producer tried to steal it outright that I realised that I had really created something of value.

The first of the two producers who actually made the film was Jonathan Shteinman. He was a friend who had occasionally slept on my couch in Los Angeles. Jonathan had worked at the Australian Film Finance Corporation, so he had a thorough understanding of the financing process, and yet no young filmmakers would trust him as a creative producer. When he asked about the status of *Angel Baby* we agreed that if he would negotiate the legal issues (it was under option to another producer), and guarantee that I would be the director, he could produce it.

REWRITING

It is my experience that most assessors and supervisors practise a form of 'tough love'. No one ever tells you they love your work.

We began rewriting the screenplay under the guidance of the Australian Film Commission. Victoria Treole, our project officer, was supportive and helpful. It's always nerve-racking when you get script notes from a stranger. What if they turn out to be idiots? Luckily, there were no idiots to circumvent. Similarly, the Film Finance Corporation (FFC) had some very valid feedback.

The triumvirate of power at the FFC connected with the Film Fund that year was John Morris, Catriona Hughes, and Errol Sullivan. Errol was the head of Southern Star Films, assigned by the FFC to handle the film fund films, better known in the industry as the 'chook raffle'. John Morris and Errol Sullivan were not terribly excited about the project. The chook raffle had not so far been a great success, and the selection process was always under attack by disgruntled elements in industry. They had short-listed *Angel Baby* with about six other projects, but it seemed that no one was terribly excited about any of them except for Bill Bennett's *Spider & Rose*. That project was fast-tracked and had finished shooting before we began pre-production. Which left the FFC more time free to push for rewrites from the other projects. Scott Hicks took *Shine* out of the race, I think mainly over budget issues, and found his money elsewhere. Jonathan and I were grumpy about it at the time, but the process caused the screenplay to get better and better.

Jonathan's notes were general – his main concern was that the story not get too soft or middle-of-the-road. He had worked on *Romper Stomper* and was very proud of that film. Jonathan wanted the film to be tough, gritty, confronting. I agreed whole-heartedly but I had to keep warning him that *Angel Baby* was a love story and a romantic one at that.

When Timothy White came in as co-producer, I went to Melbourne and began work again. Tim's notes were extensive, particularly in the refinement of the emotional lines of the characters. Tim also encouraged me to open up the script. I had always been extremely careful not to write scenes with big crowds or complex logistics. As one of the producers, Tim told me not to worry.

Louis Nowra was the original assessor for the Australian Film Commission. After reading *Angel Baby*, he told the commission that he would rather become its script editor. Working with Louis was a real pleasure for me because he was so successful and confident of his abilities, he had nothing to prove. I could summarise his contribution in three ways.

Louis has a very quixotic mind that is stimulated by the inventive and original. It was the elements that seemed conventional and pedestrian that he struck at. A lot of these had to do with the character of Harry's brother, Morris and his wife Louise. I had always thought that these characters were important to ground the audience and give them a 'normal' point of view to balance the heightened reality in which Harry and Kate lived. Louis thought that the film was always going to be about Harry and Kate, and as it turned out, he was right. As wonderful and brilliant as the performances of Colin Friels and Deborra-lee Furness were, the finished film focuses very squarely on the two main characters.

Louis also pushed me to slash the dialogue. He would go through each pass with a pencil (as opposed to a red pen) and cut most of the scenes by a third. I would defend some lines, acquiesce to others and negotiate on the rest. If the intention of a line wasn't clear, but I needed a character to react, then I would come up with a more concise way to do it. This was exciting because I had never really experienced a 'collaboration' before, and the dialectic of our argument always produced a synthesis of ideas that I could not have arrived at alone.

The third contribution was a direct result of his generosity. This was very intense emotional material, I would often find myself struggling to pull thoughts and feelings out of myself which were very personal. Some of our sessions had the structure of therapy, and I felt in safe hands as I probed my own inner life to get to the truth of these characters.

The shooting script differs significantly from the finished text of the film. This is primarily because I encouraged a lot of improvisation from the actors. I would walk onto the set for blocking and not even refer to the screenplay. I would say to myself and sometimes out loud to the actors 'Look the writer isn't here. We are. We have to make this work. We have to make it real, and true and compelling'. So we'd start the blocking with some improvisations. If I hadn't written the screenplay, I would never have had the guts to be that ruthless, but in this case I was the absolute expert on the subject of this story. Most of the time we'd come back to the text, but it gave the performances an integrity which I think shows in the finished film.

THE SET UP

The anecdote that I still find amusing is to do with the setting up of Harry and Kate's relationship. No one questioned why Harry should fall in love with Kate: 'She's beautiful, she's mysterious, she's a Goddess!' It's not a question men tend to ask. But when it came to why Kate should love Harry, we were much less sure: Jonathan, Tim, Louis and myself spent weeks arguing this back and forth. There was a good ten pages of scenes showing Harry court Kate. It was too long, but no one felt confident about cutting any scene.

We kept saying 'Maybe we won't need this, but what if we do?' The film was under scheduled and if we could have cut ten pages, everyone would have felt much more relaxed about the logistics of the shoot. But no one wanted to cut anything from the set-up of the story. I think it boils down to this fact: men do not understand why women are sexually attracted to men, or why they should fall so devotedly in love.

We even asked the editor, Dany Cooper for her 'female perspective'. Unfortunately, the editor overrode the female and Dany said, 'You should shoot it all.' Which is exactly what an editor should say. After all, if its not on film, there's no amount of fancy editing that can save it.

As it turned out, this was exactly the material that was cut from the film. The protracted courtship was cut to a very quick montage – Harry and Kate meet, they bond over their scars, physical and emotional, Kate gets her message from 'Wheel of Fortune', they make love, case closed. A lot of this has to do with the 'chemistry' between John Lynch and Jacqueline McKenzie. They are such good actors, they did their job so well, that it is impossible not to believe them as lovers. One review put it very well to me – they created a level of vulnerability and connection that was 'skinless'. But I can't help smiling at the idea of four men, all married or in long term relationships trying to puzzle this out.

THE ENDING

The history of the film's ending is a good microcosm of the evolution of ideas from page to screen. Its particularly important for two reasons. The first is that most Americans readily admit that, had it been made in Los Angeles, the film would probably not have its current ending. And the second is that many distributors and exhibitors who admire the film have found the ending makes it too difficult a marketing challenge.

I have to confess that when I first wrote the climax, I had the same feeling. 'I can't put an audience through all this shit and not give them something to feel good about.' So in my initial version, Harry, Kate and Astral lived happily ever after. There was a fundamental problem with this because I did not want to suggest that they had been 'cured' and the fact was that the doctors were spot on when they warned the lovers that their baby had a high probability of inheriting their illness.

The first version ended with Harry and Kate taking the baby back to the Drop-In Centre to show it to their friends. The last image was Astral, in the arms of her parents, surrounded by a sea of mad faces. I thought this struck the right note: a superficially buoyant ending, overshadowed by a very black cloud as we contemplated the future of this child. A writer friend exclaimed 'But Michael, that ending! It's *Rosemary's Baby*. I actually didn't think that was a bad thing, but it wasn't my intention. I was already feeling too much responsibility to the sufferers and their families to treat these characters in too reductive a fashion.

I was faced with a few problems: How would we know Astral would be all right? What sort of support system would be in place? I had one very naff version where we see Harry and Morris building a granny flat on the back of his property, the implication being that they would all live as one happy extended family. But as Tim White pointed out, 'Poor Morris and Louise. Why should they have to sacrifice their privacy?' Everything in their characters and relationship said that they would not be able to tolerate this scenario, nor would anyone judge them for that. Another equally awful idea was that the film would be framed as a story told by Doctor Norberg to a client contemplating a similar decision. In the end, the client is awe struck and asked 'What happened to the child.' Norberg introduces the client to a young psychiatrist called Astral Goodman -- apparently she grew up free from her parents illness...

In one of our key meetings with the trio of power at the FFC, all three agreed that they did not want to make a film in which schizophrenics went off their medication, became fugitives from the law, had babies and lived happily ever after. They wanted to make a film that was socially responsible and truthful. Suited me fine. I had been raised on films of the seventies – Hollywood's golden era where heroes either died or were morally destroyed *Cuckoo's Nest, Dog Day Afternoon, Midnight Cowboy, Looking for Mister Goodbar, Don't Look Now, The Godfather 1 & 11, The Deer Hunter, Raging Bull* etc. etc. Those were the days.

I called the psychiatrist who had been so supportive during my research, Dr. Chris Amanson in Los Angeles. I was nervous that he would think we were trying to get emotional mileage out of the plight of the mentally ill. I asked him, 'If you could have any ending you wanted, what would it be?' He replied, 'I would like an ending where the characters don't actually die as a result of their mental illness. Mentally ill people get hit by trucks too, you know.' Flashes of *Easy Rider* went through my mind but my sense of dramatic irony was too strong. I thought, 'What if Kate's delusional fears about losing her blood turned out to be true?' I talked to my friend who was acting as an unpaid obstetrics consultant. She was reluctant but admitted that it was possible for a mother to haemorrhage to death in labour, especially if they refused to have a Caesarean. Not likely but possible. Good enough.

I wrote various scenarios showing how Harry would survive without Kate. I even had a resolution in which Harry, who is living with Morris and Louise, sits down in front of the TV with baby Astral and 'talks' to Kate by asking questions during 'Wheel of Fortune'. But still no version was completely satisfying.

Then one day I was sitting with Jonathan Shteinman and our friend Jonathan Green, who was a young producer enrolled at the film school. Green's suggestion was that Harry, consumed with grief, join the audience at a taping of the game show, pull out a machine gun and kill everyone there, then commit suicide. While Shteinman told Green he'd been hanging around film students too long, I began to think. It had never occurred to me that Harry might kill himself. Suicide was a common enough problem faced by people tormented by voices. I immediately came up with the scene on the bridge – Harry was on the railing, squawking like a seagull – a big truck wipes by and Harry is gone. It was subtle, evocative, and brought back the other seagull scene, giving a greater feeling of narrative cohesion. We were all excited.

When Louis Nowra read the new ending, he was not as effusive. 'No, no, it just doesn't feel right. This is their story. No matter what happens.' Point taken. So I quickly wrote another version in which Kate appears beside him. I used the same dialogue as on the first 'seagull' scene. I was happy to reference this important scene because this is where the lovers' ethos is most explicitly stated, 'Shall we do it? Because now I know what peace is, I wouldn't want to stay here without you.' Tim said, 'Normally, I hate this kind of thing, but it works here.' I was more excited. How could it have ever been any other way?

The FFC hated it. They wanted us to shoot an alternative ending. Maybe Harry is gone from the bridge, but the camera pans across to the road where Harry has joined a waiting Sam and baby Astral. I didn't like that, but I was prepared to do the *Rosemary's Baby* version. As it turned out, we didn't have the money or time to shoot alternative scenes.

As we approached shooting, Jacqueline McKenzie, who could make the phone book sound like believable dialogue, came to me frowning. This was one of a couple of scenes she didn't feel comfortable with. 'I don't know. It sounds too ... literary.' 'I know what you mean, but I think it'll work.' That was my brilliant direction. Almost a year later, when we were doing ADR, Jack said to me, 'It's funny – that's the best moment in the whole film.' Maybe it's because the seagull squawking is so unliterary. I have no idea, but its since made me cautious about being too rigid in the dialogue I write.

The next factor was the logistics of shooting the ending. It was critical to get right. We had to know that the character was really on that bridge, thus the big crane shot which rises over John Lynch's head and spins around to a final close up. People often remark on that shot and it makes me worry that it actually might distract from the story. But I still don't know how else I could have done it – any other way would have looked like a cheat. And yes, John really was on the bridge. The biggest single problem was getting permission to shoot on the West Gate Bridge. It is, after all, part of a freeway and we had to block off two lanes of traffic. This was compounded by the fact that we wanted to stick an actor standing on the rails. People really do jump off that bridge and die so it wasn't exactly great PR.

I was convinced it would never happen and did a major scout of every bridge, overpass, building top etc. Luckily, the First Assistant Director, Euan Keddie decided to make it a priority to get the West Gate. He took on the responsibility himself, writing letters, explaining everything on a need-to-know basis, liaising with the powers that be, making sure that we were thoroughly organised. We had exactly three hours to shoot the wide shots on the bridge. The hot heat shot turned out well, which was just as well, because there was no going back.

The part that turned out to be the most problematic was that of Harry vanishing as a truck whipped by. We had to get two identical looking semi-trailers to drive by, with enough time in between so that John Lynch could jump off the rail and run out of the shot. Then we would just cut out the middle bit and do a quick dissolve to mask the fact there were two trucks. John was actually standing on a platform built straight out from the rail at camera height, so through the lens it looked like he was on the railing. We had been up on the bridge and realised the trucks actually had to be on the opposite side to Harry in order wipe the frame and hide the fact that Harry didn't fall past the railing. We had timed this in a practice run on the bridge and Euan worked out the timing.

We arrived at four in the morning and began shooting after sunrise. We got the shots, although Ellery Ryan, the Director of Cinematography, was concerned that the light was changing too rapidly. Ellery had also wisely suggested that a boat be set up and cued through the frame as we did the big crane shot, otherwise it would have been a pool of blackness with no sense of perspective.

When the editor, Dany Cooper, put the scene together, she first showed me a version where Harry does not vanish from the bridge. The last thing we see is Harry and Kate, then it just cuts to black. It worked well. When I saw the version where Harry vanishes behind the truck, I immediately realised it didn't work. For one thing, he 'popped' off the screen because, even with the truck masking his body, you'd still see part of him falling. Secondly, it was Louis Nowra's original point – the last image had to be of the lovers together. We played around with various cuts of the ending, but Dany's first cut was always the best and that was what went into the film. I think a good piece of cutting is as creative as a piece of music or a painting, and there was an unconscious power in Dany's work that could not be analysed – you just knew – as if it could never have been any other way.

The irony is that the audience is usually split on whether Harry jumps or not. And I am often praised for my courage in leaving it open ended. As if my intention, my 'vision' had been to create just that effect. I can never tell them the truth because it will ruin the mystery of the experience. It goes to show how most people do not understand the process of collaboration and accident, and explains why directors always get so much more credit than they deserve.

WRITING & DIRECTING

Orson Welles said, and I think he was quoting someone else, that directing movies is the 'presiding over accidents.' And now that I've done it once, I think this is the best definition. There are so many people involved in the collaboration, so many screw-ups, happy accidents, limits on time and money, so many variables, that is amazing how much credit the director is given.

In the case of *Angel Baby*, I was writer/director and I find it hard to differentiate the roles. From the first character sketches, to the writing, to the rewriting, to the workshops, rehearsals, blocking, shooting, editing, sound editing to the final mix, the job seemed to be about the same questions: Who are these characters? What is this story about? How can we best express these ideas?

The most fun I had was when something unexpected would happen in a take. An actor would throw in a line or a reaction that would make the whole thing seem so much more real or true. It was a real thrill to watch incredibly talented actors and technicians breath life into the screenplay. Show me things I'd never seen before. I would sit in front of the monitor and literally giggle with delight. Sometimes I'd have to walk off the set because I'd been made to cry. Crying and laughing has nothing to do with the job of directing, but I mention it here to show how much satisfaction I got out of the experience.

For me, directing was a blast. A dream come true. Writing is a much more painful, lonely, difficult process. Its exactly like homework. You wake up every day and you have to write. If you don't write today, you've only got to face it tomorrow. Sometimes I'll get a little thrill – I'll write a great scene, come up with a great line, find an elegant solution to an impossible problem. But compared to directing, those moments are few and far between.

Still, I believe that writing is the most important element in the process. You can do nothing without a script. Sure, a good director can elevate ordinary material. A bad director can wreck great material. But for me, its the characters, themes and ideas expressed on paper where most of the work happens.

Los Angeles, July 1996

Love Beyond the Edge

Anna Maria Dell'oso

A romantic drama about a schizophrenic couple who set up house together and decide to have a baby amid messages from chaos, *Angel Baby* was the most outstanding Australian feature film release of 1995.

Not only did it clean up seven AFI Awards – including Best Director and Best Original Screenplay for Michael Rymer, Best Actress for Jacqueline McKenzie and Best Cinematography for Ellery Ryan – but it proceeded to win most of the major categories in the Film Critics Circle of Australia Awards the following month. Early in 1996, *Angel Baby* opened in London as the centrepiece to the Tooheys Australian Film Season, collecting rave reviews. *The Guardian* newspaper summed up critical opinion by praising *Angel Baby* as a 'a cult status film that was brilliantly performed and extraordinarily daring, while its debut director, Michael Rymer, was described as 'an exceptional prospect ... [his film] manages to marry popular, approachable film-making with an acute sensitivity and a pugnacious anger.'

The emergence of a number of films with common themes or styles over a particular period of time is a testimony to the mercurial but collective nature of film-making, where creative energies dip heavily into the fleeting movements of a *zeitgeist*. In the year before *Angel Baby's* release came *Priscilla, Muriel's Wedding* and *All Men Are Liars*, Australian films linked by a camp comedic style, cross-dressing/ drag/ spectacular costumery, distinctively Australian city-country tensions and retro-pop soundtracks (two ABBAs and an Elvis). While not everyone will agree that these films should be bracketed together, overall they do have a synergistic energy, a similar flavour.

Angel Baby, with its unflinching eye for the tragi-comic, its sharp cinematography of cold surfaces and the architecture of an impersonal metropolis, and its themes of love's labours risked, came as a startling contrast. Everything about *Angel Baby* gets you where it hurts. A love story set at the membranes of psychosis and sanity, the film has the alarming schizoid beauty of a Sylvia Plath poem, only warmer and without the overtly suicidal intensity (at least at first). It's also often very funny, although the way this film's comic mood drains off into tragedy reflects the crisis of the final scenes (which features one of the most accurate and emotionally powerful portrayals of emergency labour I have seen).

Unfolding against the background of a psychiatric halfway house, *Angel Baby* shares some of the sensibilities of Mark Joffe's film version of Louis Nowra's *Così*, particularly in its warm comic opening. The lead characters, Harry (Lynch) and Kate (McKenzie) are seen affectionately amongst a quirky, tightly-knit community of people the outside world would call 'crazies'.

At this stage, these people could have been transferred off the set of *Cosi* and vice-versa (Colin Friels features in both). Indeed Louis Nowra is credited as the script editor on Rymer's film and if you look carefully enough, you'll find each film has a pivotal scene about slashed wrists, a poignant show-and-tell which depends on the same technical information about the difference between violence, self-mutilation and suicide. But the films quickly set off in opposing directions – *Così* takes the comic road as an ensemble of 'putting on a show' which stays mostly within the world of the mental institution, while *Angel Baby* turns into an ever-darkening love duet as Harry and Kate try to live together and create a family in the outside world.

In both films there is a complex thematic treatment of mental illness, using madness to illuminate the psychopathology of a fragmenting society. And as in Jocelyn Moorhouse's *Proof* (where the protagonist is a blind photographer) and *Lillian's Story* (also concerned with mental illness, women and society) there is in *Angel Baby* a sense of madness as the perceptual flaw that ironically enables the sufferer access to a way of being and thinking that is denied or repressed in the so-called sane. To a greater or lesser degree, all these films criticise the poverty of Logos when it is practised as an excessive and controlling rationality.

Australian films like *Annie's Coming Out* and *Lorenzo's Oil*, which concerned physical illness/disablement and society's lack of compassion, were heroic stories of the 'individual against society' and 'against all odds' type. *Angel Baby* is not. The mundane outside world of suburbia, work and family is not perfect but its sense of purpose and connection is still something to which the highly marginalised Kate and Harry aspire. Their struggle is all the more profound because they are treated realistically, with a mixture of sympathy and anxiety by the well-meaning but imperfect human beings around them. Everyone acts from the best motives so that *Angel Baby* is not about two misunderstood lovers fighting a heartless medical and psychiatric bureaucracy. There is no scapegoating; every act has real consequences, each choice has its price on the wheel of fortune. Nor does *Angel Baby* have a Mental Health Week agenda in explaining schizophrenia, valid and useful as such films can be. Instead the schizophrenia in *Angel Baby* is an accepted environment, a complication in the lives of the characters, who are always intensely themselves, rather than examples of psychotic behaviour.

'Love set you going like a fat gold watch,' says Sylvia Plath in a birth poem from *Ariel*, and that's exactly what happens when Harry falls for Kate at group therapy sessions conducted by Dr Norberg (Robyn Nevin). After a fearful, almost hostile response to Harry's interest, Kate becomes more receptive after they show each other their scarred wrists. A favourable omen from a game show, *Wheel Of Fortune*, seals the relationship, as Kate depends upon secret cryptic messages from her guardian angel figure, touchingly called Astral, whom she believes talks to her through the song titles and phrases that appear on the show.

So with the blessings of the music of the spheres, they fall in love without reservations or game-playing, convincing Harry's brother and his wife (Colin Friels and Deborra-lee Furness) that they can responsibly set up house together. When Kate declares they are pregnant with Astral – celebrated through wonderfully intense scenes of sacred sex and supernatural communion – the couple are awed and ecstatic. Not so their guardians and psychiatrists, even before they realise that Harry has decided he and Kate must stop taking their medication to make sure Astral is born drug-free.

We're never sure whether this is an act of transcendent love or manic insanity as the film darkens from hope to fear. Rymer's script is an electric piece of writing, full of sustained subtextual images of blood, voices, birth, death, cutting, melding and separation and an inexorable fate that works as much through *Wheel of Fortune* as the medievalists' great wheel of life. Rymer crafts a love story of unblinking directness that goes beyond courtship (portrayed in hungry sex scenes that have a raw edgy vitality to them) into love's creativity and aspirations. There is something alchemical about this couple's need to create the magical third element between them – and the fact that this angel baby is sending them messages through a TV games show every night is a poignant variation on the feeling most parents have that their children's origins are as mysteriously spiritual as they are the result of sperm meeting ova.

Director of Photography, Ellery Ryan, has an excellent eye for picking out the coldness in Melbourne's landscape and architecture, with the camera circling around bridges, shopping malls, construction sites and half-built apartment blocks of this Anytown Anywhere. But none of this would mean as much without the extraordinary performances of Jacqueline McKenzie and John Lynch (*In The Name of The Father*). Together they have a skinless quality, as if they are missing whatever it is that insulates people from the random static and madness of the universe. They are unforgettable as the lovers and so exposed through a range of emotional states that it's only later you realise this is not so much acting as a walk hand-in-hand above a precipice without a net.

Strongly supported by Colin Friels, Deborra-lee Furness, Robyn Nevin, David Argue, Geoff Brooks and Jane Menelaus, *Angel Baby* is an extraordinary debut feature from US-trained young Australian director Michael Rymer. It is one of those rare films where you come out with a great deal more than when you walked in, as its harrowing miracle climax finds an echo in Plath's last poems: 'O love how did you get here ? ... You are the one solid the spaces lean on, envious.'

January 1996

MAIN CAST [in order of appearance]

Harry	JOHN LYNCH
Kate	JACQUELINE McKENZIE
Morris Goodman	COLIN FRIELS
Louise Goodman	DEBORRA-LEE FURNESS
Sam Goodman	DANIEL DAPERIS
Dr Norberg	ROBYN NEVIN
Dave	DAVID ARGUE
Rowan	GEOFF BROOKS
Frank	HUMPHREY BOWER

Produced by Timothy White and Jonathan Shteinman
Written and directed by Michael Rymer
Complete film credits appear at the end of the book.

PRINCIPAL CHARACTERS

HARRY, late twenties, client at psychiatric daycare centre
KATE, twenty-two, fellow client and Harry's lover
MORRIS Goodman, late thirties, Harry's brother
LOUISE Goodman, late thirties, Harry's sister-in-law
SAM GOODMAN, five, Harry's nephew
DR NORBERG, thirties, supervising psychiatrist at daycare centre
DAVE, twenty, friend of Harry's, client at centre
ROWAN, fifties, friend of Harry's, client at centre
FRANK, forties, friend of Harry's, client at centre

How this Script Relates to the Screen Version

The '✱' symbol indicates that Scenes 34, 35 & 37 were montaged together to form parts of Scene 23 in the finished film.

Curly brackets around text indicate dialogue or scene descriptions that were edited out during the production process.

Scene 38 from the pre-production script was cut from the film so has no final film version scene number.

SCENE 34   EXT. CEMENT CANAL – NIGHT   {23 ✱}

Harry and Kate slide down the concrete bank. {*They come to a point where water flows down the bank from a tunnel above them. Harry laughs nervously as Kate scrambles up the bank towards the tunnel, but follows reluctantly.*}

SCENE 35   INT. CEMENT CANAL/TUNNEL – NIGHT   {23 ✱}

{*The water roars around them. Kate leans against the wall and reaches up under her dress to pull down her panties.*} *Harry steps closer, pressing against her. Kate wraps her arms around his neck and helps him lift her up. Slowly, he lowers her down. They both sigh, then continue to move together.*

SCENE 36   INT. CLUBHOUSE/MEETING AREA – DAY   {24}

Norberg is doing her best to solicit some response from the medication-heavy clients. Kate and Harry sit opposite one another, bored by the experience. They exchange an ever-so-subtle raise of the eyebrow.

SCENE 37   EXT. STREET/FREEWAY UNDERPASS – DAY {23 ✱}

Kate and Harry stand in the shadows of a doorway making love as if they had never stopped.

{SCENE 38   EXT. ROOFTOP – NIGHT

This time they've found an old mattress, but it's still not the most comfortable place to make love.

SCENE 1   EXT. CLOUDS/CITY STREET – DAY

1

Title music begins and opening credits roll as we float by a giant white cloud, like a sheer ten-storey cliff of cotton wool. We move down into the open space where high clouds cast shadows on an ethereal plain of clouds below. We soar down towards the snowy plain. Wisps of cotton wool pass close by and we are completely immersed in white. The white turns to grey as we descend into a much moodier atmosphere of dark storm clouds. Thunder rumbles as we descend, emerging on the rainy side of a summer storm. We descend through the heavy rain, passing the flashing lights on the antennas on sky scrapers. We pass the flat modern patterns of glass and concrete as we boom down through the skyscrapers towards the street where a lone figure, Harry, in his late twenties, stands in the street, mouth open, eyes closed, his face tilted towards the sky. He shakes his head, and wipes his eyes, then glances at his watch. Realising he is late, he curses to himself and takes off down the street.

SCENE 2   EXT. BUS STOP – DAY

2

Three strange characters stand under the shelter of a bus stop: Rowan, in his fifties, carrying a portable black-and-white TV; nerdish Dave, twenty, and tall Frank, in his forties, who has a five-mile stare and talks quietly to himself. They all have two things in common: They have deep, dark circles around their eyes and they dress like shit. A bus approaches. They shuffle their feet impatiently and look around with growing anxiety as the bus pulls to a stop in front of them. Harry races down the road from the opposite direction.

ROWAN: Harry!
DAVE: Where have you been?
HARRY: Sorry, Dave. Come on Rowan.

> *Harry has to lead Rowan up the bus steps, the TV getting in the way, as the bus driver gives them a tired, familiar look.*

[*To the bus driver*] Hang on ... [*To Frank*] Frank!

> *Harry leads Frank onto the bus and jumps on just as the impatient driver pulls away.*

SCENE 3   INT. BOWLING ALLEY/COUNTER – DAY   {3}

Harry is busy trying to organise Dave, Rowan and Frank into their bowling shoes. The lane manager looks on.

HARRY: What's your shoe size?
DAVE: Twenty.
HARRY: That's your age, Dave. You're not a twenty.
DAVE: I am!
HARRY: [*to the lane manager*] Give him a ten. [*To Dave*] Twenty it is for Big Foot here. [*To Frank*] What about you, Frank?

> *Frank just goes on mumbling.*

SCENE 4   INT BOWLING ALLEY/LANE – DAY   {4}

{*Harry is now helping his friends choose bowling balls.***}**

HARRY: Don't get your fingers stuck in the holes, now.

> *Rowan throws the ball up in the air. It bounces down the lane and actually makes contact. Harry, Rowan and Dave cheer while Frank mumbles.***}**

> *Dave throws the ball full force. The ball drops in the gutter, sending him into a temper tantrum.*

> *Frank stands very still, mouthing words. He makes some strange signs to himself then casually tosses the ball, turns and sits down. The ball strikes out. Harry is astonished.*

> *Rowan throws again. But this time the ball almost stops and just dribbles into the gutter. Rowan starts walking down the lane. Harry looks up from his score sheet.*

{HARRY: Hey Rowan, where you going?
DAVE: Rowan, you moron!**}**

> *The lane manager steps down to their lane.*

LANE MANAGER: [*shouting*] Hey you! Get back here!

Rowan cowers and continues towards the pins.

{You hear what I said?}
HARRY: It's okay, it's okay. I'll get him back.

Harry goes down the lane after Rowan.

{LANE MANAGER: Hey!}
HARRY: [*striding away*] Rowan, {c'mon.
ROWAN: I gotta get my ball.
HARRY: The ball comes back. Your ball is already back down there.}

Rowan looks doubtfully at Harry. Suddenly, a ball comes hurtling towards them. Harry has to leap out of the way.

HARRY: That's not funny, Dave!
LANE MANAGER: [*walking towards Dave*] Okay, that's it. Get out!
DAVE: [*suddenly aggressive*] Fuck you.
LANE MANAGER: What did you say?

Chaos sets in as Dave cackles hysterically. Harry rushes back, putting himself between Dave and the Manager.

SCENE 5   INT. CLUBHOUSE/MAIN AREA – DAY   {5 �֍}

The 'clubhouse' is an informally structured daycare centre for the mentally ill who are not ill enough to be institutionalised. Psychiatric clients move about the large open space, which is equipped with a kitchen, tables, chairs, couches, a pool table, stereo, etc. The walls are decorated with hand-made signs and charts: 'Balance Your Diet', 'Job Applications', 'Emergency Numbers & Services'. The room is filled with about forty clients in all shapes and sizes. They all have the same dark circles around their eyes. {Harry follows Dr Norberg, in her thirties, the supervising psychiatrist worker of the clubhouse, towards her office.

DR NORBERG: Harry, the employment agency called this morning.
HARRY: [*remembering*] Oh, yeah …
DR NORBERG: That was your second appointment.
HARRY: Don't worry about it. It's all part of my master plan.

DR NORBERG: What plan is that?

HARRY: Well, I have this theory that important events always occur in threes. The third appointment, I'll blow 'em away.

DR NORBERG: You're ready now, Harry.

HARRY: [*changing the subject*] Hey Vicky, how about we go out tonight?

DR NORBERG: What about your girlfriend?

They glance over at a plump girl, Georgia, sitting in the corner of the main room, wearing five sweaters, a woollen ski hat and gloves.

HARRY: Too many layers. I like a woman to dress for easy access.

Dr Norberg smiles and shakes her head as Harry follows towards her office.

Okay, so we'll bring her along; she can drool in the corner ...

Dr Norberg gives him a warning glance and gently shuts the door to her office.} Harry steps away and watches through the observation window as Norberg greets a small East Indian man, Dr. Singani, who is with a new client – a pale, thin girl of twenty-two: Kate. Dr Norberg tries to engage Kate in conversation, but she just rolls her eyes, making it clear that she doesn't belong here. Harry stands transfixed.*

SCENE 6   INT. CLUBHOUSE/CONFERENCE – DAY   {9}

Harry sits in a circle with several other clients from the clubhouse. Norberg ushers Kate to a seat.

DR NORBERG: Kate, this is Brendan, Joanne, Dave, Rowan, Maria and Harry.

Kate couldn't care less. She puts down her large carpetbag, sits, and pulls out a cigarette.

We have a custom that the new person tells something about themselves.

Kate looks up, realising she is expected to speak.

KATE: Kate.

> *Everyone waits expectantly.*

My name is Kate.

> *Dr Norberg nods and waits. The other clients look blank. But Kate has no intention of saying anything more. She drags on her cigarette and looks them all in the eye. Harry leans back, watching her with great interest.*

DR NORBERG: Okay, thank you Kate. Anyone else like to jump in?

> *Harry's point of view: Dr Norberg's voice fades out even as her lips continue to move. Kate sits with her arms crossed, her eyes raised to the ceiling, lost in thought. Harry focuses on the long scars on the soft part of her forearm. She notices and covers herself.*

{SCENE 7   EXT. MORRIS' HOUSE/STREET – DAY

A bus pulls away to reveal rows of ordered houses with manicured homes. Harry bounds up the road, over the lawn and into one of the houses.}

SCENE 8   INT. MORRIS' HOUSE/KITCHEN – NIGHT   {6}

Harry sits at the kitchen table eating dinner with his bearish brother Morris, and Morris' down-to-earth wife, Louise, who is still wearing her tailored suit from a hard day at the office. Both are in their late thirties.

HARRY: She's a Goddess. She's beautiful, and fiery and mysterious. I worship her.
LOUISE: Why doesn't anybody ever say that about me?
MORRIS: [*avoiding Louise*] Where does she come from?
HARRY: I don't know. We haven't actually talked yet.

> *This stops them short. Harry goes on eating merrily. Their five-year-old son, Sam, comes out, half-asleep in his pyjamas. He reaches out and finds his mother's lap.*

LOUISE: What are you doing up, sweetheart?
SAM: There's monsters in my room.
LOUISE: Sam, go back to bed.
HARRY: I'll do it. [*To Sam*] So where are these monsters?

> *Harry winks as Sam leads him off to his bedroom. Morris grins*
> *but Louise is not pleased.*

LOUISE: Morrie ...
MORRIS: You try getting Sam back to bed that fast. He's fine.

SCENE 9   INT. MORRIS' HOUSE/SAM'S BEDROOM
– NIGHT   {7}

The room is filled with kids' toys, a painting of a clown and another of
a puppy dog: the kind of stuff a kid would never pick for himself.
Morris and Louise stop in the doorway to listen as Harry tucks Sam
under the covers.

SAM: They laugh at me and they keep getting closer.
HARRY: Where do they come from?

> *Sam points towards the closet. Harry nods seriously. He picks up*
> *a piece of chalk from Sam's miniature blackboard sill.*

You know what this is? This is a special piece of chalk that
keeps away monsters. Look ...

> *He squats down and traces a semicircle on the hardwood floor*
> *around the door to the closet. He takes a handful of chalk and*
> *places it on Sam's night table.*

This'll last you for weeks. Make sure this line isn't broken
before you go to bed and you'll be safe as houses.

> *Sam snuggles down. Harry kisses him, switches off the light next*
> *to the bed, and heads for the door. The light switches back on.*

SAM: Uncle Harry.
HARRY: Mmm hmmm.
SAM: There's a monster there.

> *He points to the clown painting. Harry takes it down and frowns.*

HARRY: I see what you mean. Are you sure this is the only one left?

Sam nods. Harry lifts the window, tosses the painting out and shuts the window. Sam sits up, squealing.

Shhh! Go to sleep or you'll get us both in trouble.

Harry switches off the light.

{SCENE 10   EXT. MORRIS' HOUSE/DRIVEWAY – NIGHT

Harry wheels the rubbish bin down the driveway. A neighbour across the street is doing the same thing. The neighbour glances at Harry and retreats back up his drive way without a word. Harry shrugs to himself and walks across the lawn, grabbing the clown painting off the grass as he goes.

SCENE 11   INT. MORRIS' HOUSE/MAIN BEDROOM – NIGHT

Morris lies flicking through the channels while Louise reads a magazine.

MORRIS: What do you want me to do? I can't kick him out.
LOUISE: What about the boarding house?
MORRIS: You're worried about Sam.
LOUISE: No ... he's imagining some pretty weird stuff.
MORRIS: He's a kid.

SCENE 12   EXT. MORRIS' HOUSE/PATIO – NIGHT

Harry pauses, holding the painting, listening to their conversation.

LOUISE: [*off screen*] I know.

Pause.

Just so I know, how long do you think Harry'll need to stay, this time?

Harry goes inside through the sliding doors.}

SCENE 13   INT. MORRIS' HOUSE/BATHROOM – NIGHT   {8}

There several lists taped to the wall, neatly printed in coloured felt pens: 'MEDICATION: Morning: 2 Serenace, 1 Benztropine – Lunch: 1 Serenace – Dinner:2 Serenace, 2 Benztropine. THINGS TO DO: take medication – brush teeth – shave ñ shower – wash underwear'. Harry stands before the open medicine cabinet, which is lined with bottles of pills. He takes two pills from one bottle, two from another, then one from a third bottle. He shuts the cabinet and downs the pills with a glass of water, staring at himself in the mirror.

SCENE 14   INT. CLUBHOUSE/MEETING AREA – DAY   {5 ✿}

A nature documentary plays on the TV mounted up in the corner while several clients sit watching and chain-smoking. Kate sits alone on a couch writing in an exercise book. Rowan lines up the cue ball and breaks like a pro. **{***He continues his run while Harry stands holding his cue, watching Kate. Harry casually wanders over to the TV area and stands behind Kate. He tries to peer over her shoulder. We get a glimpse of a page covered with neatly printed dates, numbers and phrases in tiny handwriting. We swish back as Kate slams the book shut and turns to glare at Harry.*

KATE: You want something?
HARRY: Hi, I'm Harry...

> *Harry waits for her to respond. Kate just stares at him over her shoulder, waiting for him to leave. Harry gets the hint, and raises his arms apologetically. He backs off and she slowly re-opens her book and goes back to the TV.***}**

SCENE 15   EXT. CLUBHOUSE/BUS STOP – DAY   {10}

Kate stands waiting for the bus. Harry approaches from behind. He tries to think of something to say, but the bus arrives.

SCENE 16   INT. BUS – DAY   {11}

The bus is deserted. Harry shows his pass and follows Kate to the back. He sits across the aisle, but then she stands and moves several seats away. The bus comes to a stop, the doors open and another passenger boards. Suddenly Kate stands and exits just as the doors are shutting. Harry rushes after her and rattles the doors.

DRIVER: Hey! Get back from that door!

SCENE 17   EXT. STREET – DAY   {12}

Kate walks briskly down the street with Harry following her.

SCENE 18   EXT. STREET/DOORWAY – DAY   {13}

Kate turns a corner, then breaks into a sprint and dives into a doorway. Harry turns the corner and walks down looking for Kate. He stops outside a dark entrance. Kate steps out into the street feeling stupid.

KATE: Are you one of these weirdos who follows women home?
HARRY: This is the first time.
KATE: I don't hang with psychos, okay?
HARRY: I'm no psycho.
KATE: What are you doing at the clubhouse, then?
HARRY: Nothing. Same as you.

> *Harry is looking at the scars on her wrist. Kate's look is so dark that Harry takes a step back.*

Who cut you?

> *Kate flinches and glares at him furiously.*

{KATE: Keep away from me!

> *Kate takes off down the street, leaving Harry kicking himself.*

SCENE 19   EXT. SOCIAL SECURITY OFFICE – DAY

We hear a montage of sounds from the city's radio signals – telephone calls and electronic codes – as the sun beats down and we tilt down between the high rise buildings, the billboards. The montage fades out as we move down a sparse modern plaza to Harry and Rowan, who smoke cigarettes. Harry sits with his head against the wall, eyes closed, while Rowan frets beside him. A mix of disabled people, pensioners, and some clients from the clubhouse fill the background.

ROWAN: [*anxious*] Where's my number ... ?
HARRY: It's right here ...

Harry fishes into Rowan's pocket and pulls out a numbered plastic card. We continue to track across to the glass doors of the social security office as the sound of a screaming fight draws our attention. The door flies open as Kate is carried out by a burly office worker in his forties.

KATE: Go fuck yourself!
OFFICE WORKER: Oh, that's charming language.

The burly office worker drops her on the pavement but she is instantly on her feet, punching and kicking him with fury.

KATE: Gimme my cheque!
OFFICE WORKER: You heard the lady. Your file is still in transfer. Come back tomorrow.

He is forced to grab her arm and twist it back so that she screams. Harry can't help himself: he races up and grabs the office worker's other arm.

HARRY: Let her go.
OFFICE WORKER: Keep out of it!
HARRY: Let her go.

Furious, the office worker releases his grip on Kate. Immediately, she starts kicking and punching again, only this time Harry is the recipient of her blows.

KATE: Fuckheads! Give me my cheque!

Harry cowers and tries to protect himself as the office worker shakes his head and leaves them to it.

HARRY: Hey! Stop that ... Stop that!

Harry has to grab Kate around the waist and pin her arms, but still she tries to kick him.

KATE: Let go of me.

> *Harry drops her on her arse and backs away, rubbing his arms.*

HARRY: Jesus Christ ... !

> *Kate gets up, looks around at the line of people staring, then straightens her clothes and walks quickly down the street.*

SCENE 20   EXT. SPIRAL STAIRCASE – DAY

Harry jogs up beside Kate who is stomping down the street. She glances at him without slowing her stride. Harry falls in beside her.

KATE: Stop following me!

HARRY: Jeez, are you paranoid or what? Rowan had to pick up his cheque, so I...

> *Harry shrugs.*

KATE: [*remembering*] Shit, my cheque ...

> *Still walking, Kate pats her pockets. Harry pulls out a pack of cigarettes and offers her one. She takes a handful and puts them in her pocket.*

HARRY: You need some money?

KATE: [*sarcastically*] No, I don't need some money. [*Softening*] Thanks for the cigs. I'll pay you back sometime.

> *They walk on a few moments in silence.*

HARRY: You hungry?}

SCENE 21   EXT. UNDER A BRIDGE – DAY   {14}

Kate and Harry walk away from a hot-dog stand. Kate rips open the aluminium paper and inhales the hot dog in several gulps. Harry struggles to keep the conversation alive.

HARRY: You live around here?

> *Kate gives him a warning glare.*

KATE: I'm staying at this hostel.

HARRY: I'm staying with my brother's family.
KATE: How nice for you.
HARRY: I get in the way. Families are okay, though.

> *Kate shrugs.*

KATE: They took me away from my father when I was still young
'cause he raped me.

> *Harry stares at her as she casually licks her fingers clean of
> mustard. Harry gives her his hot-dog and she takes it without
> hesitation.*

HARRY: [*innocently*] What was it like?
KATE: [*nonchalant*] Like death.
HARRY: I always figured death was more peaceful.
KATE: Ever see anyone die?

> *Harry shrugs and smiles. Kate regards him with increasing
> curiosity.*

How did you know someone cut me?

> *Harry takes her arms and traces along the scars.*

HARRY: If you did it yourself, they wouldn't be down like that;
they'd be straight across, like this.

> *Harry pulls down his sleeves and shows Kate the scars on his
> wrists. Kate looks with interest, chewing her hot dog. Suddenly
> she stops with her mouth full.*

KATE: Oh, shit ...
HARRY: What?
KATE: I gotta go.

> *She shoves the rest of the hot dog in her mouth and takes off
> down the street.*

SCENE 22   EXT. STREET/BUS STOP – DAY   {15}

*The bus pulls away in a black cloud of exhaust. Kate sprints after the
bus but trips and falls to the ground, winded. Harry catches up, also
winded, and tries to help her but she bats him away.*

HARRY: You okay?
KATE: You ... ! You made me late!
HARRY: Late for what?
KATE: [*furious*] I gotta find a TV! {Just forget it. You wouldn't understand.}

Harry gets an idea.

HARRY: Come with me.

He grabs her arm but she shakes free.

[*Continuing*] Come on

Harry drags Kate down the street by the hand.

SCENE 23 EXT. STREET/FOOTBRIDGE – SUNSET {16}

Harry and Kate run across the bridge towards the lights of the city.

SCENE 24 EXT. STREET/APPLIANCE STORE – NIGHT {17, 23 ✲}

{*They run down an alley.*

KATE: Let go! I missed it already.
HARRY: [*pointing*] Look.

Across the street is an appliance store with a dozen television sets in the window. Through the window, we see Kate approach as if she were in church. She gets out her note-book and opens it to the last entry. Harry steps up behind her, watching her, not understanding.} *Through the glass, on the TV screen, Adriana Xenides turns the letters on the board.*

{You ever wonder why they need her to turn the letters?
KATE: [*suddenly angry*] Adriana is fabulous!
HARRY: Don't flip out. I like Jeopardy myself...
KATE: Just shut up.}

Through the glass, on Wheel Of Fortune, *a contestant solves the puzzle 'Postage Stamp'. Kate jots it down.*

HARRY: Why do you write down the puzzles?
KATE: 'Cause I have to, or I won't get my messages.
HARRY: Someone's sending you messages.
{KATE: Don't tell anyone.
HARRY: Who'm I gunna' tell?

> *Harry considers.*

What about all the other people who watch the show?
KATE: Look, if I go on the TV and tell you specifically, Harry
    meet me at the usual place and time, would the ten million
    other people watching know what I meant?
HARRY: [*trying to see the connection*] No ...
KATE: Well, it's the same with} Astral. She sends me messages no
    one else can understand.
HARRY: Who's Astral?

> {*Kate doesn't answer.*

KATE: Forget it.

> *A beat.*}

Astral's my Guardian Angel. Don't you laugh at me.
HARRY: I believe you.
KATE: I don't care if you believe me or not.
HARRY: What kind of message is 'Postage Stamp'?
KATE: That depends on the question.
HARRY: Oh.
KATE: Think of a question.

> *Harry thinks about it, gets the question clear in his head and nods.*

HARRY: Okay. Should I tell you?
KATE: You don't have to.
HARRY: I asked if you and me were going to be together.
KATE: You can't do that.
{HARRY: Why not?}

> *On the TV screen, 'A TITLE' is the clue. Several letters are
> turned but the answer is not yet obvious. 'YO_ A_ _ MY
> SP_ _ _A _ AN_ _ _'*

KATE: {You tricked me.
HARRY: Could be 'Bridge Over the River Kwai' for all I know.

> *They concentrate on the screen, mouthing possible answers.*

'You ... ate ... my ... spegal Andes'.
KATE: What the hell is that?

> *Kate looks at him, puzzled. Harry shrugs. Kate can't help cracking a smile. On the* Wheel of Fortune *two 'L's are turned.*

Two 'L's ... 'special' ... 'angle' ... No, 'angel'.} [*Excited*] 'You Are My Special Angel'.

> *Harry starts to sing the song. {Kate is surprised, but can't help singing along even though she doesn't know the lyrics. Harry helps her along and they finish on the chorus, Harry throwing his arms out in a parody of a crooner. But when he turns back to Kate, he realises that she is no longer singing. Kate studies his face, frowning.*

HARRY: [*uncomfortable*] What are you looking at?

> *She doesn't answer, just keeps looking at him. Harry smiles and turns away, embarrassed, but when he looks back, Kate is still watching him. Gradually, he overcomes his self-consciousness and faces her, looking into her eyes.}*

SCENE 25   EXT. STREET/FOOTBRIDGE – NIGHT   {23 ✼}

> {*Harry and Kate walk back towards the bus stop, each lost in their own thoughts.*

KATE: You've got special powers, don't you?
HARRY: I'm pretty good at focusing my elementals.

> *Their hands brush. Kate tentatively takes Harry's hand as they walk. They stop and}* Harry darts at Kate, kissing her smack on the lips. He backs off to see her reaction. {*Kate looks a little spooked, so he doesn't persist. She turns and walks away. Harry stands, watching her go, completely infatuated, overflowing with excitement. He does a little dance in a circle, then throws*

up his arms. The river of lights flows on, while Harry stands with his arms raised victoriously.}

{SCENE 26   INT. KATE'S HOSTEL/STAIRWELL – NIGHT

(Note: in the film Scene 26 is replaced with an exterior scene at the hostel in which Kate knocks on the door and is admitted by Rose.) Kate runs up the stairs past some other clients hanging around the lobby and entrance hall. The hostel manager, Rose, in her fifties, a big matronly woman, stands on the landing above her. Kate averts her eyes and moves past, up the next flight.

ROSE: Kate, you're very late tonight.

> *Rose follows, speaking with the infuriating 'reasonableness' of a social worker.*

KATE: I missed the bus.
ROSE: It took *two hours* for another bus?

> *Kate rolls her eyes and goes into her room. She starts to shut the door but Rose is right there.*

You know I'm responsible if anything happens.

> *Kate flashes with anger but gets herself under control with a deep breath.*

KATE: I'm sorry I was late, Rose.

> *A beat as Rose swallows Kate's defiant tone.*

ROSE: That's okay, Kate.}

SCENE 27   INT. KATE'S HOSTEL/KATE'S ROOM – NIGHT
{19}

We can hear whispering as we pan across the walls, which are covered with clippings of Adriana and Wheel of Fortune *from* TV Week. *We continue panning to a small home-made altar, complete with candles, and framed photograph of Adriana in the centre, stopping on Kate who kneels, praying with intense concentration.*

KATE: [*whispering, scared*] ... Please Astral, tell me so I can know for sure ...

> *(Note: in the film, Scene 27 is followed by a montage of Scenes 24, 25, 33, 34, 35, 37 and also includes a shot of Harry lying alone on his bed. The sequence traces the developing relationship between Kate and Harry.)*

{SCENE 28   INT. CLUBHOUSE/MEETING AREA – DAY

It's 'activities time' and Harry leans over Rowan's shoulder as he sits staring suspiciously at an out-of-date computer terminal.

HARRY: It's not trying to hurt your brain. It's just a computer. Look, you just move the mouse ...

> *Harry leans over and moves the mouse.*

ROWAN: Don't!
HARRY: Okay!

> *Rowan moves the mouse and blinks in surprise. Harry shakes his head as if to clear out Rowan's mental static. He stops as something catches his eye. On the other side of the room, there's a long table filled with clients, clipping coupons from the newspaper with great industry. Kate sits at the end looking at the other clients frowning. Harry pats Rowan on the shoulder and starts to move towards Kate when he is intercepted by Dave.*

DAVE: Listen, we have to talk.

> *Dave shuffles his feet looking unusually sincere. Harry continues watching Kate.*

HARRY: What's on your mind?
DAVE: Look, I hate to do this to you, but Georgia and me are in love.

> *Harry's point of view: Kate is looking around at the other clients' scissors with apprehension. She tries to rip her newspaper by hand, but the whole operation is a mess.*

HARRY: Who?

DAVE: Georgia!

> *Dave points over to Georgia who is sitting bundled up in her twenty-five scarves.*

We've been meaning to break the news for a while but we didn't want to destroy you.

HARRY: [*distracted*] That's fine, Dave ...

> *Harry walks away. Kate is carefully ripping the paper, which attracts some curious stares from the other clients. Harry approaches and sits beside her.*

How's it going?

> *Kate is rigid with self-consciousness. Harry reaches across her and picks up a pair of scissors.*

Try these...

> *Suddenly Kate scrambles sideways, knocking the client beside her.*

CLIENT: Hey, watch it!

> *Kate cowers like a frightened animal, attacked from both sides. Harry is taken by surprise. He moves towards her, still holding the scissors. Kate screams and scrambles away, barrelling through another client, sending the whole immediate area into an uproar.*

Help! Stop her!

> *Dr Norberg and another assistant rush in from different directions.*

DR NORBERG: Kate! Kate, what's the matter!
KATE: No! No!

> *The assistant tries to grab Kate from behind but she writhes and screams at him. The other clients start to move around, agitated, as if infected by the same psychosis.*

DR NORBERG: [*to Harry*] What happened!

Harry shrugs helplessly, then looks at the scissors. He tosses the scissors on the table and holds up his hands. Kate stops struggling, but continues hyperventilating with those wild eyes. Harry looks helplessly as Norberg and the assistant usher Kate into her office.

SCENE 29   EXT. STREET/CLUBHOUSE – DAY

Kate moves down the street, hugging herself, feeling awful. Harry runs up beside her and falls into step.

HARRY: I'm sorry, I don't mean to ...

They walk on in silence.

Everybody freaks out sometimes ...

KATE: It's weird ... It's like I'm watching myself become this freak, but I can't stop it ...

They stop. Harry doesn't know what to say.

Don't you see it's no good? I – I – I – can't even trust myself. How am I ever gunna trust anybody else?

Harry draws her to him and wraps his arms around her. At first she tenses up, then, as he holds her tighter, she relaxes and begins to sob into his chest in terrible spasms of pain. Eventually, she pulls away and wipes her nose and eyes with her hand.

HARRY: Here, use mine.

He helps her wipe her face with his own sleeve. Kate can't help smiling. Harry smiles back. But suddenly, Kate's smile is replaced by another look of fear.

Hey, hey, what's wrong?

KATE: How do we know this is for real?

SCENE 30   INT. WON KOK RESTAURANT – NIGHT

The owner, Mr Chin, comes out from the kitchen to where Harry and Kate are waiting, and takes out two menus. The first drops of rain begin to splatter the window outside.

CHIN: Cookies aren't for sale. You get cookies when you order food.

Harry and Kate look at each other hopefully, but neither has any money.

HARRY: Please. It's just one little fortune cookie.

CHIN: No, you go away.

HARRY: It's a matter of life or death.

Chin gives them a strange look.

CHIN: [*groans*] Aaah, okay.

Chin disappears into the kitchen and comes out carrying a large cardboard box.

Your hands clean?

Kate holds out her hands for inspection. Chin nods then offers her the box. Kate digs her hand in deep and pulls one out. Nervously, she hands it to Harry. Harry takes a deep breath, cracks it open, and reads the message. Kate waits, trying to gauge his reaction. Harry hands her the message.

The message reads 'You will be lucky in love'. They look at each other with real heat. Chin is embarrassed. Kate impulsively grabs Chin across the counter and kisses him on the cheek. Harry grins and pumps his hand enthusiastically.

HARRY: Thank you. Thank you, very much.

SCENE 31   EXT. WON KOK RESTAURANT – NIGHT

It has now started to rain steadily. As Kate and Harry exit hand in hand Chin shuts the door and pulls the shade. They walk to the edge of the curb and stop. They kiss, unable to wait any longer. And kiss and kiss and kiss ...

KATE: Where can we go?

HARRY: My nephew's room is right next to mine.

KATE: We can't go to mine.

Suddenly Kate breaks away, leaving Harry leaning forward in surprise. Staring at him with steady eyes, Kate leads him by the hand into the alley around the corner.}

SCENE 32   EXT. ALLEY OFF STREET – NIGHT   {23 ✱}

{Harry and Kate move down the dead-end alley scanning around for shelter. Now Harry takes the initiative and draws Kate into the shadow of the dumpster.} Their hands begin to reach under clothes, exploring the contours of the other's body.

{KATE: We should be realistic about this.
HARRY: What have we got to lose?
KATE: Our minds.
HARRY: We've already lost that.

Suddenly, there's a loud crash. Mr Chin heaves a second bag of rubbish into the dumpster. He stops and glares as Harry and Kate emerge from beside the dumpster looking hot and bothered.}

SCENE 33   INT/EXT. STREET/PHONE BOOTH – NIGHT
{23 ✱}

We push in on the isolated phone booth, rain streaming down the sides –– Harry and Kate are squeezed in, kissing, trying to negotiate the difficult task of undoing buttons in the tiny space. He hitches her dress while she fumbles with his pants.

{HARRY: I'll get a job and find us a place with a bed and sheets.
KATE: I don't want to wait that long.

A solitary figure sprints through the rain towards the phone booth, his coat pulled up over his head for shelter. Seeing Harry and Kate, he stops and stares. Harry glances up and stops. The man stares in at him, bewildered and fascinated. Harry grabs at his pants and stops Kate who is carrying on oblivious. Harry and Kate exit the phone booth and run into the night, the man still staring after them.}

SCENE 34   EXT. CEMENT CANAL – NIGHT   {23 ✻}

Harry and Kate slide down the concrete bank. {They come to a point where water flows down the bank from a tunnel above them. Harry laughs nervously as Kate scrambles up the bank towards the tunnel, but follows reluctantly.}

SCENE 35   INT. CEMENT CANAL/TUNNEL – NIGHT   {23 ✻}

{The water roars around them. Kate leans against the wall and reaches up under her dress to pull down her panties.} Harry steps closer, pressing against her. Kate wraps her arms around his neck and helps him lift her up. Slowly, he lowers her down. They both sigh, then continue to move together.

SCENE 36   INT. CLUBHOUSE/MEETING AREA – DAY   {24}

Norberg is doing her best to solicit some response from the medication-heavy clients. Kate and Harry sit opposite one another, bored by the experience. They exchange an ever-so-subtle raise of the eyebrow.

SCENE 37   EXT. STREET/FREEWAY UNDERPASS – DAY {23 ✻}

Kate and Harry stand in the shadows of a doorway making love as if they had never stopped.

{SCENE 38   EXT. ROOFTOP – NIGHT

This time they've found an old mattress, but it's still not the most comfortable place to make love.

SCENE 39   INT. MORRIS' HOUSE/UPSTAIRS HALLWAY – NIGHT

Louise switches off the kitchen light and heads towards her room with a bedside drink. She stops at Harry's door and opens it.

SCENE 40   EXT. PARK – NIGHT

Harry and Kate cling together, approaching climax behind a broad tree. Kate cries out, pushing forward. They fall and land heavily, rolling together on the damp ground.

SCENE 41   INT. MORRIS' HOUSE/LIVING ROOM – DAY

Louise comes out from the corridor with an armful of dirty laundry and continues out to the service porch. She passes Harry and Sam who are sitting in front of the television together.

LOUISE: [*off screen*] Harry, I picked up the laundry off your floor.
HARRY: [*calling out*] Louise, please don't do my laundry!

> *Harry gets up to follow her, but Sam leaps on his back, dragging him back down to the ground.*

SCENE 42   INT. MORRIS' HOUSE/LAUNDRY – DAY

Louise is busy loading the washing machine.

LOUISE: [*calling*] I have to put on a load anyway ...

> *She stops and looks at one of Harry's shirts. It is caked with mud and covered with grass stains.*}

SCENE 43   EXT. MORRIS' HOUSE/BACK YARD – DAY   {25}

Chicken sizzles on the BBQ. Morris stacks a few pieces on a tray and carries them to the picnic table where Louise is already helping Sam cut up his food. Harry comes out from the kitchen carrying a jug of cordial and some plastic glasses. Louise keeps giving Morris prompting looks as they settle, serve each other salad etcetera. Harry hovers over the table, stuffing his face with his fingers. Sam watches Harry, wondering how he gets away with it.

MORRIS: Harry ...

> *Harry stops.*

HARRY: Yes?
MORRIS: [*lost for words*] How are you doing?
HARRY: [*chicken in mouth*] I believe I'm fabulous.
LOUISE: So where do you go every night?

> *Harry is astonished. He starts to laugh uncontrollably, which is not the most reassuring thing for Morris and Louise.*

HARRY: I've fallen in love.

> *Now it's Morris and Louise's turn to be astonished. Sam looks around, enjoying the show. Finally, Morris breaks the silence with a grin.*

MORRIS: You old dog, why didn't you tell us?
HARRY: She's nervous about meeting you.
LOUISE: Is it the girl from the clubhouse?
HARRY: That's her. She's a client.

> *Harry smiles and digs into his food. This news does not thrill Louise, but Morris is genuinely pleased.*

SCENE 44   EXT. KATE'S HOSTEL – SUNSET   {26}

A very unappealing, sterile building with a few resident clients sitting on the steps outside.

SCENE 45   INT. KATE'S HOSTEL/KATE'S ROOM – SUNSET
{27}

Kate kneels in front of her floor-length mirror, putting on make-up and earrings. She stands and smooths down her dress, then takes a deep, nervous breath.

SCENE 46   EXT. KATE'S HOSTEL/STAIRWELL – SUNSET {28}

Harry paces around the hallway while the residents sit watching TV in the adjoining lounge. Kate descends the stairs in a pair of stilettos, wearing a dress that's perhaps a little too colourful and too tight. The residents give Kate a round of whistles and catcalls. Rose, the hostel manager, steps out of the kitchen to check out the noise. She is surprised to see Kate so dressed up.

HARRY: Wow ...
KATE: I'm too dressed up.
HARRY: You look fabulous.

> *Kate flushes with pleasure at the compliment. But Kate's smile fades as she sees Rose frowning up at her with disapproval. Harry*

*offers Kate her arm. Kate gives Rose an aloof glance and wobbles
out the door on her heels.*

SCENE 47   INT. BUS – NIGHT   {29}

*Kate and Harry sit on the bus, attracting strange looks from the other
passengers. Kate seems strangely agitated.*

SCENE 48   EXT. MORRIS' HOUSE/FRONT DOOR – NIGHT
{30}

*Kate and Harry walk up the drive way towards the looming house.
Kate stops dead.*

HARRY: What?
KATE: I don't know if this is a good idea.
HARRY: Kate, I need you.
KATE: [*snorts*] You don't need me.

> *Harry pauses with his hand on the door.*

HARRY: I do.
{KATE: I'm about to pee my pants.}

SCENE 49   INT. MORRIS' HOUSE/HALLWAY – NIGHT   {31}

Harry opens the door and they enter. Kate stares around her in awe.

HARRY: [*calling out*] We're here!

> {*Louise calls out from the half-open door to her room.*

LOUISE [*off screen*] I'll be right out!
KATE: [*nervous*] This is really nice.

> *Morris comes in from the kitchen wearing an apron.*

MORRIS: Hey, you're here.}
HARRY: Morrie, this is Kate. Kate, Morrie.

> *They shake hands uncertainly. Kate lunges forward and pecks him
> on the cheek. Morris is surprised but he decides he likes it and
> laughs. Kate laughs, relieved that she hasn't done the wrong thing.*

KATE: Can I use your ladies' room?
MORRIS: It's at the end of the hall.

> *Kate smiles and backs out towards the corridor. Morris watches her go.*

You met *her* at the clubhouse?

> **{***Louise comes out from her bedroom, buttoning up her dress. She walks into the bathroom.*

SCENE 50   INT. MORRIS' HOUSE/BATHROOM – NIGHT

Louise comes face to face with Kate who is sitting on the toilet.

LOUISE: Oh, um ... I am so sorry.

> *Louise goes to shut the door.*

KATE: That's okay, I'm done.

> *Kate stands up and smooths down her dress. She smiles and holds out her hand.*

Hi, I'm Kate.

> *Louise takes her hand and glances down.*

Whoops ...

> *She laughs, reaches down and pulls up her pants.***}**

SCENE 51   INT. MORRIS' HOUSE/KITCHEN – NIGHT   {32}

The foursome sit eating their dinner which happens to be roast chicken. Harry and Kate shovel their food with uninhibited abandon. Kate pauses and decides to negotiate her chicken. She takes her spoon and tries to slice through her drumstick, but it slips and bounces off her plate. She glances around nervously, picks it up, puts it back on her plate, then tries again. Morris and Louise watch this ordeal while trying not to stare. They look at Harry to see if he notices anything, but he stuffs his face, oblivious.

SCENE 52   EXT. MORRIS' HOUSE/BACK YARD – NIGHT {33}

Louise and Kate sit on the suspended couch taking in the night air.

{*Through the window, Morris and Harry can be seen washing dishes over the sink.*}

KATE: You have a fabulous home.
LOUISE: Thank you.

> *They sit comfortably in silence.*

Harry's a nice guy.
KATE: Nice isn't the word. [*Embarrassed*] But you know him much better than I do.
LOUISE: No, you're right. 'Nice' is wrong. I meant he's different.
KATE: He's the best lay I ever had.

> *Louise leans back in amazement. Kate blushes and smiles. Louise can't help laughing.*

He has this little sideways move that drives me insane.
LOUISE: Really ...
KATE: I swear, if you strapped electrodes to his nuts, you could light up the city.
MORRIS: [*off screen*] What are you two talking about?

> *Morris and Harry emerge, Morris wiping his hands.*

KATE: Just girl talk. [*To Harry*] Did you tell him?
HARRY: Not yet.
MORRIS: Tell me what?

> *Harry smiles and rolls his eyes.*

HARRY: Kate and I are moving in together.

> *Harry and Kate laugh at their stunned expressions.*

KATE: We've started looking for a place to live.
HARRY: We have two pension cheques to keep us going ...
KATE: Until we get jobs. Harry's going to get a job as a computer whatsit and I can make a few bucks doing something.
HARRY: Well? Say something.
MORRIS: Wait a second. Give us a minute to adjust, here.
HARRY: We already talked to our shrinks about it. They like the idea as long as we show up to therapy.

KATE: And take our medication.}

Louise and Morris think about it more seriously.

LOUISE: I think it's a good idea.

Morris takes a longer moment. He shrugs.

MORRIS: Yeah.

Kate throws her arms around Morris and Louise.

KATE: [*relieved*] I was so afraid you'd say 'No'.
MORRIS: I'm gunna give you something to help you get started.
HARRY: Thanks, but we decided that we're going to do it alone.
MORRIS: Come on, let me help you.

Harry looks to Kate and she nods and smiles. {*They turn to each other appreciatively and kiss.*

HARRY: Have you ever seen me so happy? }

SCENE 53   INT. HOUSING COMMISSION OFFICE – DAY{34}

The Commission officer, a matronly woman with large butterfly glasses and a tailored suit, flips through a book of Polaroids and stats on various layouts.

COMMISSION OFFICER: There's a one-bedroom in the north tower on the fifth floor.
KATE: What's the actual address?
COMMISSION OFFICER: [*surprised, reading*] Twenty-five Charlotte Street.

Kate turns to Harry who scratches out some figures on a small notepad.

HARRY: [*to Kate, under his breath*] It's a seven. We need something more solid, like a four or an eight. [*To the Commission officer*] No good.
KATE: Do you have anything else?

The Commission officer blinks, not understanding what's going on.

COMMISSION OFFICER: Okay ... there's a limit of three choices. [*Reading*] There's a one-bedroom in the west tower on the fourth floor.
KATE: What's the address?
COMMISSION OFFICER: Sixty-two Anderson Lane.

Harry makes some notes ...

HARRY: Perfect.
KATE: Does it have a window facing East?

The Commission officer stares at them suspiciously: are they making fun of her?

{SCENE 54   INT. HARRY AND KATE'S APARTMENT – DAY

Morris wanders around the dingy one bedroom place while Kate waits expectantly.

MORRIS: How much is it?
KATE: [*walking around*] We're going to put a table here. And the living-room over here.
HARRY [*off screen*] Hey, Kate, come and look at this!

Kate runs into the bedroom. Morris drags his finger across the wall, leaving a mark.

MORRIS: How much is it?
COMMISSION OFFICER: A hundred a week.
MORRIS: A hundred? For this?
COMMISSION OFFICER: You try finding a place where the address adds up to a four and there's a window facing east.

They are interrupted by the sound of Harry and Kate squealing and giggling in the bathroom.}

SCENE 55   EXT. HARRY AND KATE'S BUILDING/WALKWAY – DAY   {36}

Kate carries a sack of laundry over her shoulder. She stops and knocks on a door which opens and another sack is passed out. She heaves them both on her shoulders and struggles down the stairs.

SCENE 56   EXT. HARRY AND KATE'S BUILDING– DAY   {37}

Kate emerges from the entrance, now balancing an enormous load of laundry. She walks quickly down the street looking like an ant carrying a crumb twice her size.

SCENE 57   INT. LAUNDROMAT – DAY   {38}

Kate loads the laundry into a heavy-duty drier, then slips a couple of coins into the slot.

SCENE 58   INT. HARRY AND KATE'S APARTMENT – DAY{35}

(Note: the filmed scene contains significant differences.) We start on a colourful hand-made quilt, then move across the neatly kept living room, past the piles of folded linen stacked on an ironing board against the wall, stopping on Harry. He sits wearing a business suit inherited from Morris, reading a library book and smoking a cigarette. Kate, wearing one of Morris' tacky barbeque aprons, refills his coffee cup and uses great concentration to slice a tomato with a large spoon. Harry watches without comment.

KATE: What time is your appointment?
HARRY: Five o'clock. You can watch it on 'Wheel of Fortune'.
KATE: Ha, ha. Did you take your medication?
HARRY: I stopped a couple of days ago.
KATE: [*incredulous*] Why?
HARRY: I'm sick of going to job interviews looking like a zombie.

   Kate sits down, frightened.

KATE: I could never do that.
HARRY: I couldn't have two months ago.
KATE: [*relaxes*] I guess anything's possible huh?

SCENE 59   INT. HARRY AND KATE'S APARTMENT – DAY{40}

On the TV, Wheel of Fortune *is in progress. The audience applauds as the wheel spins and gradually stops.*

JOHN BURGESS: Two-fifty.

CONTESTANT: I'll take a 'T'.
JOHN BURGESS: We have a 'T'

> *More enthusiastic applause as Adriana turns over the letters on the board. Kate sits propped up on an old four poster bed studying the television and jotting notes on a pad. The pad reads: 'Q?: HARRY'S INTERVIEW'.*

{SCENE 60   INT. PERSONNEL OFFICE/WAITING ROOM – DAY

Muzak filters from the ceiling vents. The fluorescent lights buzz. Harry sits pretending to read a magazine. He glances around at the daunting number of applicants. The door opens and the boss's personal assistant appears. Harry leaps to his feet with enthusiasm, strides across the room, stops and races back for his briefcase.

PERSONAL ASSISTANT: Mister Rabinoff.

> *One of the applicants rises and walks past Harry into the office. Harry sits down, embarrassed.*}

SCENE 61   INT. HARRY AND KATE'S APARTMENT – DAY 61
                                                                    {42}

Adriana turns over the remaining letters. Kate jots down the clue: 'A person: scatterbrain'.

KATE: That's obvious. But what about the interview?
JOHN BURGESS: We have time for one more round and the clue is a phrase.
KATE: Okay, here we go.

> *The wheel spins ...*

SCENE 62   INT. PERSONNEL OFFICE/BOSS'S OFFICE – DAY
                                                                    {41,43}

The clicking of the wheel continues as the audience applause fades out. The executive director, a distinguished grey-haired man in his fifties, wearing a suit, sits across his desk studying Harry's resumé.

EXECUTIVE DIRECTOR: Everything looks fine. Since the time you left IBM, where were you employed?

HARRY: I was in hospital.

EXECUTIVE DIRECTOR: Do you mind me asking what was wrong?

HARRY: It was my hearing.

EXECUTIVE DIRECTOR: What about after? That was almost two years ago.

HARRY: Oh, I've been consulting for different companies, designing specialty software for the mentally disadvantaged, interactive learning programs, that sort of stuff.

The executive director looks impressed.

SCENE 63   INT. HARRY AND KATE'S BUILDING/LOBBY– DAY   {44}

Harry runs into the elevator.

SCENE 64   INT. HARRY AND KATE'S APARTMENT – DAY{45 ✳}

Harry enters through the front door and stops. The blinds are drawn and the room is filled with candles. The door swings shut and Kate steps up behind him, naked, and nuzzles his neck.

HARRY: You know already?

KATE: [*chewing away*] The clue was 'A phrase'. The answer was 'Roll out the Red Carpet'.

> *Harry starts getting horny. He reaches behind him and takes hold of her naked waist. He turns her around and runs his hands up and down her back. She breaks free, runs into the kitchen and emerges with a bottle of cheap champagne.*

HARRY: [*impressed*] Champagne.

She hands him the bottle and he uncorks it awkwardly.

KATE: I got the one with the plastic cork.

Harry fills their jars and they raise them.

To your new job.

HARRY: To our new life.

> *Harry and Kate drink and fall into another kiss. Kate casually spills her champagne down Harry's back, causing him to shout in shock. Kate just giggles and helps him strip off. They fall onto the bed and begin to make love.*

SCENE 65   INT. HARRY AND KATE'S APARTMENT – NIGHT
{45 ✸}

A candle burns. Harry opens his eyes and stares blankly, taking a moment to orient himself. He tries to move and suddenly realises that he is bound, hand and foot, to the posts of the bed. He struggles to get free but the cords holding his ankles and wrists only tighten.

HARRY: Kate!

> *Kate comes out of the bathroom and crosses to the kitchen. Harry watches as she drops strange plants and roots into a big pot of boiling water.*

Kate! Why am I tied up?

> *She drops to her knees at the end of the bed.*

This is not funny.

KATE: I'll untie you, but you have to give me an oath that you'll be mine.

> *Harry struggles as Kate crawls forward.*

You'll only hurt yourself.

> *The cords cut into his skin. He cries out.*

I told you. Promise me. Promise me now.

> *They are nose to nose.*

HARRY: I give in. I'm yours.
KATE: I didn't hear you.
HARRY: I, Harry Goodman, promise that I'll be yours 'til the hour, 'til the second of my death.
{KATE: And then?

HARRY: For the rest of eternity.**}**

> *Suddenly Kate darts away and runs into the kitchen. She fills the jar with a very dubious looking liquid.*

Kate? Come on, I said it ... Let me go.

> *Kate comes back and holds the jar to his mouth.*

KATE: Drink it.
HARRY: What is it?
KATE: Drink it!

> *Harry opens his mouth, expecting the worst. She gently tips the liquid into his mouth. He winces from the taste but keeps drinking.*

HARRY: What is it?
KATE: Just a little love potion to make sure.

> *Kate unties his arms and legs. He leaps to his feet and rubs his wrists.*

HARRY: What the hell was that about?
KATE: We're pregnant.

> *Harry stops short.*

HARRY: We are?

> *Kate nods and waits for his reaction.*

Are you sure?

> *She pulls out her notebook and flips through the pages.*

KATE: Last week. Look at the bonus rounds for each day.
HARRY: 'A title: "Joy to the World"'.

> *Kate flips the page.*

Another title: 'Great Expectations'.

> *She flips another page and thumps down with her finger.*

KATE: 'A phrase: "Big as a Blimp"'.
HARRY: So you haven't actually been to a doctor.

KATE: No doctors; all they want to do is cut you open. No doctors.

HARRY: Shouldn't you do a test or something?

KATE: I have all the symptoms: nausea, vomiting, big tits. Besides, my period's late.

HARRY: How late?

KATE: Two months. [*Before he can react*] I was waiting 'til you got a job to tell you.

> *Harry sits down, stunned.*

Harry? Are you okay?

SCENE 66   INT. HARRY AND KATE'S APARTMENT – NIGHT
{46}

Kate and Harry lie in bed staring at the ceiling. He does some calculations in his head.

KATE: Harry?

HARRY: Yeah.

KATE: What are we going to do?

HARRY: We're going to have a baby.

> *Kate turns to Harry.*

KATE: Really?

HARRY: Really.

{KATE: You really mean that?

HARRY: Yeah.}

> *Kate rolls over and leaps on top of Harry, smothering him with hugs and kisses.*

SCENE 67   INT. CLUBHOUSE/RECEPTION AREA – DAY   {47}

> *Morris and Louise enter and approach the front desk where one of the clients, Joanne, a heavily medicated elderly lady is acting as receptionist.*

JOANNE: Can I help you?

MORRIS: Is Doctor Norberg's office here? We have an appointment.

JOANNE: Okay, just sign in here.

Morris and Louise look at each other, spooked.

LOUISE: We're not clients.

Joanne gives them a patronising smile. Meanwhile, Harry is moving around the room, proudly stuffing cigars into his friends' mouths.

HARRY: ... There's one for you, and you and you.

He tries to gives one to Dave, but he pushes it away. Norberg is ushering Kate, Morris and Louise into her office.

DR NORBERG: [*calling out*] Harry?

HARRY: Be right there! [*To Dave*] C'mon, Dave. They cost me fifty cents a piece.

DAVE: Keep your cigar, you fuckin' sell-out.

HARRY: How am I a sell-out?

DAVE: The job, the wife, the kid, the apartment. You're a walking margarine commercial.

HARRY: And what are you?

DR NORBERG: [*off screen*] Harry ...

HARRY: Just a minute!

ROWAN: Harry, forget about it.

HARRY: No, I want him to tell me. You're here 'cause you got nowhere to go. Well, I got a home now, and someone who needs me. So fuck you.

Harry marches into Dr Norberg's office.

ROWAN: Harry ...

SCENE 68   INT. CLUBHOUSE/DR NORBERG'S OFFICE – DAY   {48}

Harry sits next to Kate, across from Morris, Louise and Dr Singani. Dr Norberg is in the midst of making introductions.

DR NORBERG: Doctor Singani, this is Morris and Louise Goodman. Doctor Singani is Kate's ...

KATE: He's not my doctor. {He can't even speak English.}

> *Harry elbows her to shut up but she bats him away.*

I told him I had butterflies in my stomach, so he writes in my file 'Patient has hallucinations of insects in abdomen'.

> *A thoughtful pause.*

DR SINGANI: Is there another doctor whom you would prefer?

KATE: Yes, Doctor Seuss.

DR NORBERG: If it's okay with you, Kate, I would prefer to have Doctor Singani stay.

KATE: You can have who you like: it's still my body.

DR NORBERG: Okay, now that we have that clear, the next question is, 'Will you see an obstetrician?'

KATE: No.

DR NORBERG: We don't really know if you're pregnant.

KATE: I told you I was pregnant.

MORRIS: [*reaching*] What about you, Louise? You went to an obstetrician, didn't you?

LOUISE: Everyone does ...

KATE: If everyone jumped off a cliff, would you?

DR. SINGANI: Assuming Kate is pregnant ...

KATE: I am in the room.

HARRY: Kate and I have already agreed that we weren't comfortable with the idea of an obstetrician ...

MORRIS: This is ridiculous ...

HARRY: [*interrupting*] That's why we went to see a registered midwife.

> *Harry pulls out a letter and hands it to Dr Norberg, who reads it.*

{DR NORBERG: Kate is ... pregnant.}

> *They all turn to stare at Kate and Harry who are being very nonchalant. Dr Singani smiles, realising he has been outwitted.*

DR SINGANI: The hormonal changes occurring during pregnancy can be stressful for a woman in complete health. The chances of a relapse into psychosis are considerably higher.

HARRY: We know that. But think of the benefits. A sense of purpose, a sense of meaning. The feelings of love and connection.

DR NORBERG: [*to Harry*] What if your voices come back?

DR SINGANI: [*to Kate*] What if you have a relapse?

KATE: I could call someone ...

> *Kate stares ahead, knowing this isn't a good answer.*

DR SINGANI: Who would you call?

KATE: Morris and Louise.

DR NORBERG: Have you asked them about this?

> *An uncomfortable silence. Morris almost interjects but glances at Louise and thinks better of it.*

What if Louise isn't home when you call?

HARRY: {Then she'll call someone else.} 'What if', 'What if' ... What if she trips and falls? What if I get hit by a truck? Bad things can happen to anyone.

DR NORBERG: There is one bad thing we haven't talked about. There's a chance that the child will inherit your illness.

{HARRY: What kind of chance?

DR NORBERG: [*shrugging*] It's not an exact science. It could be as high as forty-six percent.}

HARRY: We don't drink, we don't take street drugs, we don't beat each other up. Astral could do a lot worse. We love her already 'cause she's a special gift from God. She *chose us*.

SCENE 69   EXT. FAST FOOD RESTAURANT – DAY   {49 ✳}

MORRIS: [*off screen*] Harry, we're your family. I'm anxious about what's going to happen to you and this baby.

SCENE 70   INT. FAST FOOD RESTAURANT – DAY   {49 ✳}

Harry, Kate, Louise and Morris carry their trays through the crowded restaurant towards the window.

{KATE: [*interjecting*] Her name is Astral.}

HARRY: You think that we won't take care of Astral?

MORRIS: It's not that you won't try, but you can't control what happens to you.

They move to a table by the window.

HARRY: [*louder*]You have a family. You're in no position to tell me I can't have what you have.

Morris glances around the restaurant, embarrassed.

MORRIS: [*quietly*] You and me are not the same thing!

Harry stands, shaking with anger.

HARRY: I have the right to try. If you can't stand by us, then we can't see you any more.

MORRIS: Harry, sit down...

LOUISE: Morrie's not saying we won't stand by you. We just want to make sure you've thought this through.

{HARRY: It's going to be hard enough without your constant negative elementals. Kate ...}

Harry strides out the door.

KATE: What do you want me to do? Do you want me to have an abortion?

Kate gets to her feet and follows Harry.

SCENE 71   EXT. BRIDGE. – DAY   {50}

Harry stands silhouetted against the setting sun, dwarfed by the scale of the bridge. He climbs the rail as if to jump. Kate moves along the railing and climbs up beside him. Seagulls float above them buffeted by the steady breeze.

KATE: Should we do it?

Harry is not amused.

Now I know what peace is, I won't go back to stay here without you.

A flurry of seagulls rise in front of them, causing Kate to cry out, laughing. Harry's frown begins to soften. Kate throws up her arms as if to fly. Harry turns to watch her as she continues to flap her wings and squawk, uninhibited. Slowly, he starts to imitate her, squawking and flapping his arms.

SCENE 72   EXT. HARRY AND KATE'S BUILDING– DAY   {39}

The camera booms down to the roof of Kate and Harry's building. Kate emerges from the stairwell wearing a mini-skirt and bare feet, carrying a plastic lunch-box. She walks to the edge of the roof then kneels before an arrangement of small pots containing a rose bush, garlic bulbs and pigweed. She clips off leaves and flowers and places them into different compartments of the lunch-box, labelled with names like 'Molly', 'Rose' and 'Love Lies Bleeding'.

SCENE 73   INT. HARRY AND KATE'S APARTMENT – DAY
{52 ❋}

*{*Harry sits at the kitchen table, smoking a cigarette, lost in concentration as he makes notes from a library book. Kate unloads her lunch-box onto the table in front of Harry. She sorts out the different herbs, then grinds them with a mortar and pestle.*}

HARRY: Okay, we have to clean out our systems. No more cigarettes, [*stubbing out his cigarette*] no more coffee, doughnuts or hot-dogs. And no more medication.

   Kate does not like this last suggestion.

Kate, you don't want Astral on a Stelazine cocktail before she's even born?

KATE: What if they're right about my hormones?

{HARRY: If they're right, we shouldn't be doing this at all. Listen ... [*reading*] 'Recent studies, have shown that anti psychotic drugs occasionally cause malformations or congenital

---

* Note: in the film Scenes 73 and 74 are continuous, interior bathroom. The filmed scene contains significant differences.

anomalies in the foetus.'}

Kate is horrified by the idea.

We don't have a choice.

{*Harry races to the bathroom with Kate following anxiously behind.*}

SCENE 74 INT. HARRY AND KATE'S APARTMENT/ BATHROOM – DAY {52 ❋}

Harry crosses to the medicine cabinet behind the mirror. He pulls it open, grabs a row of orange bottles, and empties them into the toilet. {*Kate screams and dives into the bowl, grabbing at the pills. Harry pulls her back and flushes the toilet.*

KATE: What the fuck did you do that for?
HARRY: If we quit, we quit.
KATE: Not all of them!

He sees how vulnerable she is. Harry strokes her head soothingly.

HARRY: I'll protect you, I promise.}

SCENE 75 INT. HARRY AND KATE'S APARTMENT – DAY{51}

Harry and Kate sit naked, intertwined.

HARRY: Ready?

Kate nods. They interlace their fingers and place them on Kate's naked belly. The camera tracks forward as they close their eyes and concentrate.

HARRY: I'm focused in, how about you?
KATE: What do you see?
HARRY: Nothing yet; we haven't started.
KATE: Sorry.
HARRY: Focus ... Focus in. Concentrate your thoughts into a flower.
KATE: What kind of flower?

HARRY: A rose.

KATE: What colour is it?

HARRY: Pink. Stop talking, focus ... Focus in. Let the petals open up, one by one. Okay, now open the whole flower wider and wider 'til it's like a big cup between us.

The camera tilts up to the naked light bulb which flickers. Harry and Kate open their eyes.

{HARRY: I think she came down.}

Kate gasps, feeling her stomach.

KATE: Did you feel that?

Harry nods. They both wait, their hands pressed against her belly. They feel something again.

It's her. It's Astral.

{SCENE 76   INT. HARRY AND KATE'S BUILDING/LOBBY – DAY

A confusion of wires dangle from the open ceiling as an electrician tests some circuits from the top of a ladder. The elevator doors open to reveal Harry and Kate kissing.

HARRY: You be careful: don't do too much work, okay?

KATE: Okay. I love you.

HARRY: Not as much as I love you.

Harry kisses her. She pulls him close and wraps her arms around his neck, the elevator door bouncing against their backs. The electrician stops to watch. Harry has to pull away and vanishes into the lift. Noticing the electrician, Kate glares and retreats into the elevator.

SCENE 77   INT. HARRY AND KATE'S APARTMENT – DAY

Kate is busy, ironing, watching TV. There's a knock on the door. Kate freezes. There's another knock on the door. Quietly, she goes to the door and listens.

/47

~~8~~ INT. HARRY AND KATE'S APARTMENT/
~~ENTRA~~NCE – DAY

The electrician waits, holding his tray of tools. We can hear the TV through the door. He knocks again.

SCENE 79   INT. HARRY AND KATE'S APARTMENT – DAY

Kate recoils from the noise, but she doesn't move.

SCENE 80   INT. HARRY AND KATE'S APARTMENT/
ENTRANCE – DAY

The electrician leans closer, as though he can hear someone.

ELECTRICIAN: Is somebody there?

> *He shakes his head and gives up, turning back down the hall to the stairs.*

SCENE 81   INT. HARRY AND KATE'S APARTMENT – DAY

Smoke rises from the iron which is face down against a shirt. We track across the unfinished pile of laundry and stop on Kate, who is crouched in the corner of the kitchen.

SCENE 82   INT. HARRY AND KATE'S APARTMENT/
BATHROOM – DAY

Dramatic music plays on the TV from the living room. Kate takes the burned shirt and shoves it in the back of a cupboard. She stops and stares at herself in the mirror.}

SCENE 83   INT. HARRY AND KATE'S APARTMENT – EARLY
EVENING   {66 ❋}

Harry sits reading while Kate paces back and forth. The old TV plays a black and white movie in the background.

HARRY: You okay?
KATE: What's the matter with you?

> *Kate glares at him defensively. Harry realises she is genuinely disturbed.*

HARRY: [*shaking his head*] Nothing. Come here...

> *Harry reaches out and tries to grab hold of her waist, but she slaps him away.*

KATE: [*hissing*] Don't touch me!

> **{***On the TV a woman screams as the killer raises the knife and stabs. Blood flows. Kate leaps at the TV and flicks the channel. We see an advertisement for Ginsu knives.*

DEMONSTRATOR: If the knife is sharpened properly, it just slices through the flesh ...

> *Kate stares as a knife slices through a tomato. She hits the power button as if it were a poisonous spider.***}**

KATE: I want my Stelazine.
HARRY: It's the withdrawals.
KATE: Get it for me now!
HARRY: You don't need it.
KATE: Shut up, you stupid bee's dick. How the fuck do you know what I need?

> *This hits Harry like a physical blow.*

I'm sorry ...
HARRY: That's okay.
KATE: Get me my Stelazine!

> *A short pause. Harry leaps to his feet and carefully lifts Kate under the arms.*

What are you doing!

> *Kate struggles and screams as Harry carries her into the bathroom.*

SCENE 84   INT. HARRY AND KATE'S APARTMENT/
BATHROOM – EARLY EVENING   {66 ✹}

Harry lifts her, fully dressed, into the shower. She screams as he turns on the cold water, but stops struggling. Harry turns the water off and reaches out a hand. Kate slaps it away and sinks to the ground.

KATE: I've gotta have it. I'll kill myself, I swear to God.

>   *There's a knock at the door. Kate looks up, terrified. Harry*
>   *stands and starts towards the door.*

Don't!

>   *Harry freezes and they wait. There's another knock.*

LOUISE: [*off screen*] Harry? Kate, it's Louise!

>   *They stare at each other in surprise.*

SCENE 85   INT. HARRY AND KATE'S APARTMENT – EARLY EVENING   {66 ✽}

Harry pulls open the front door to reveal Louise.

LOUISE: Hi ...

>   *She waits.*

I brought a few things for Kate. Some books on pregnancy, and
some vitamins.

>   *She digs into her bag and starts pulling stuff out.*

HARRY: Come in.

>   *He shuts the door. Something catches Louise's eye: Kate is*
>   *standing in the doorway, her clothes completely saturated.*

LOUISE: Hi.

>   *Kate crosses and sits down on the couch, avoiding Louise's eyes.*
>   {*Harry grabs some towels and starts to dry her off.*}

Is everything okay?
HARRY: Everything's fabulous.
LOUISE: [*watching Kate*] Kate?
KATE: You heard him.

>   *Louise looks suspiciously from one to the other. {There's a knock*
>   *on the door. Harry and Kate look up and freeze. Louise watches*
>   *them, not understanding why they don't answer the door.*

There's another knock.

ELECTRICIAN: [*off screen*] Anyone home?
LOUISE: [*moving towards door*] Would you like me to ... ?
HARRY: [*whispering*] No!
LOUISE: Why not?
HARRY: Sshhh!
LOUISE: What's wrong?
HARRY: Nothing!

Harry catches himself over-reacting and blushes. Kate dances around anxiously. There's a long pause.

ELECTRICIAN: I can hear you in there!

Louise crosses to the door with determination.

LOUISE: This is ridiculous.}

Suddenly, Harry and Kate scramble into the bathroom. The door slams shut, leaving Louise alone in the room. {Louise shakes her head and pulls open the door. It's the electrician, wearing overalls, carrying a tool box.

ELECTRICIAN: What's wrong with you people?
LOUISE: Excuse me?
ELECTRICIAN: [*irate*] Why don't you answer the door?

The electrician goes to push past her but she blocks his path.

LOUISE: I don't think this is a good time.
ELECTRICIAN: I'm not coming back again.
LOUISE: That's fine. We'll take care of it.

Louise shuts the door in his face. She sighs and turns towards the bathroom, frowning.}

SCENE 86   INT. MORRIS' HOUSE/KITCHEN – NIGHT   {67}

Louise sits at the kitchen table with some work from the office spread out around her, while Morris empties the dishwasher.

LOUISE: Have you heard from Harry and Kate?

MORRIS: I would have told you if I had.
LOUISE: I went 'round to their place today.

> *Morris stops and looks at her in surprise.*

I was on the way home from work.

> *Morris shakes his head, pleased that she should take an interest.*

MORRIS: That's great.
LOUISE: I think we should spend more time with them.

> *Morris' smile is replaced by concern.*

SCENE 87   INT. SHOPPING CENTRE/K-MART – NIGHT
{53, 54, 56}

We track along the deserted checkout stalls to Harry and Kate, who are waiting to pay for a pram. The pimply-faced check-out boy, in his late teens, scans the label and rings up the total on the cash register.

CHECK-OUT BOY: That's sixty-nine ninety-nine, please.

> *Harry and Kate look at each other, puzzled.*

HARRY: I thought it was ninety-one ninety-nine.
CHECK-OUT BOY: It's a sale item, see ...

> *The check-out boy points out the red sale sticker on the other side of the label. Harry and Kate examine the new price, conferring in lowered tones.*

KATE: Six, nine, nine and nine is a twenty-four, which is a six.
HARRY: Six is okay, but I'd feel better if it was a one for new beginnings.
KATE: [*to the check-out boy*] We don't want the sale price. Here ...

> *She hands over ninety-two dollars.*

CHECK-OUT BOY: It's a sale item. It's reduced.
KATE: We want to pay the full amount.
CHECK-OUT BOY: I can't do that.
HARRY: Just pocket the difference. We don't care.
CHECK-OUT BOY: [*glances around embarrassed*] I can't.

KATE: Take it, you little pimple!
CHECK-OUT BOY: [*bewildered*] I'll ... lose my job. I can't ...

> *Kate starts to get agitated.*

KATE: Why won't he take our money?
HARRY: It's okay ...
KATE: What's the matter with him?

> * {*Other shoppers start to turn and stare. The floor manager looks up from behind his desk. Harry glances around embarrassed.*

HARRY: Please, go wait over there.

> *Kate snorts at him but he stares her down.*

Go ...

> *He waits.*

Please ...

> *Kate crosses her arms protectively and moves away, glaring at the check-out boy. In the background, we see a twelve-year-old rollerblader cruising down the mall outside.*}

SCENE 88   INT. SHOPPING MALL – NIGHT   {57, 59, 61 ✽}

Kate steps out from behind a column and collides with the rollerblader head-on. Close shot of Kate's leg as the buckle rips her skin. Kate and the rollerblader fall in a heap. Kate is more dazed than anything.

KATE: Are you okay? You should slow down.
ROLLERBLADER: I'm sorry, I'm really sorry ...

> *The rollerblader looks down. Blood is trickling from the rip in Kate's stocking. The rollerblader pulls a scarf off his arm and unties it. Meanwhile, Harry arrives at the scene.*

HARRY: You okay?

> *Kate looks up and nods. She feels the rollerblader touching her, turns and recoils.*

---

* Note: from this point the filmed scene contains significant differences.

KATE: Keep away from me!

>*She sees the dark blotch of her blood on his scarf.*

Give me that back.

>*The rollerblader is stunned. He pushes off, still holding the scarf.*

He's got my blood.

>*The rollerblader is now pedalling through a few scattered shoppers. Kate tries to stand.*

He's got my blood!

>*All Harry sees is the rollerblader through the mall.*

HARRY: Hey...

>*Harry rushes after him. The rollerblader clicks across the shiny floor. Harry stretches out and runs harder.*

Hey!

>*The rollerblader glances back and skates away even faster.*

SCENE 89   INT. SHOPPING MALL/OUTSIDE K-MART – NIGHT   {61 ✤}

Kate is surrounded by the check-out boy and some concerned shoppers. A middle-aged woman reaches toward Kate, offering a sympathetic hand. Kate reels backwards, breaking free.

SCENE 90   INT. SHOPPING MALL – NIGHT   {61 ✤}

The rollerblader reaches a descending section of walkway and accelerates out of control, falls, slides, and crashes into an array of cleaning equipment. Harry sprints to a stop in front of him. The rollerblader scrambles backwards, scared out of his mind.

ROLLERBLADER: I'm sorry, I didn't mean it.

>*Harry sees the expression on the boy's face and realises the whole thing was an accident.*

HARRY: Give me that.

Harry snatches the scarf from the rollerblader's hand.

SCENE 91   INT. SHOPPING CENTRE/FOOD COURT –
NIGHT   {62 ❋}

Kate's point of view: suddenly, sound is everything: the click and hum of the refrigerators, the whine of the floor polishers in the distance. Kate moves through the forest of black chairs stacked neatly on tables. The whine of the polisher is amplified and distorted a hundred times. Kate freezes and stares in front of her with a mixture of fear and fascination: the shadows of the black chairs seem to be moving. Kate spins around; more chairs are moving. No, its not the chairs, just their shadows ... We move through the rows of black chairs, their limbs sticking out like gnarled tree limbs. We turn one way, then another, but everywhere we go, more chairs. Suddenly, we whip around and Kate is standing in front of us. Kate screams at the camera and backs away, knocking over rows of chairs. They crash to the ground. More chairs crash in a chain reaction, the sound amplifying intolerably.

{SCENE 92   INT. SHOPPING CENTRE/OUTSIDE K-MART –
NIGHT

Harry runs back to the spot he left Kate but she is nowhere in sight. Several shoppers hurry through some sliding doors beneath a neon sign which reads 'FOOD COURT'. They exchange nervous laughter and look generally spooked. Harry rushes out through the sliding doors.}

SCENE 93   INT. SHOPPING CENTRE/FOOD COURT –
NIGHT   {62 ❋}

(Note: in the film Scenes 93 and 94 are continuous interior.) Harry comes through the sliding doors. He can see Kate trying to stand up amongst the confusion of chairs. {He breaks into a run. Harry tries to grab her hand but she turns on him and shoves him back with amazing strength. Her face is strangely twisted. Harry holds out his hands, trying to pacify her.

HARRY: Look Kate, I got your blood back. Look.

She sees the blood and backs away and runs out another set of glass sliding doors into the car park.

SCENE 94   INT. SHOPPING CENTRE/CAR PARK – NIGHT
{62 ✻}

Harry catches up with Kate who is trying to squeeze herself under a car.

HARRY: Kate ...

He pulls her up but she just stares at him in shock.

It's just a little cut. It's okay.

Harry tries to pacify her in his most soothing voice. He rips off his shirt and tears it into pieces.

Let me wrap up the cut so I can stop the bleeding.

Kate moves back with renewed suspicion. Harry continues to approach with the strip of shirt outstretched.

KATE: It's my blood. We can't go home, Harry, they've got my blood.

Kate stops moving as she realises what's happening to her. She starts to rub her sides.}

I can't feel my body. Help me, Harry ...

That's all the encouragement he needs. He approaches her with arms outstretched.

I can't feel my body.
HARRY: Feel me.

Kate touches his back, then presses her hands in. Harry squeezes her tight. Kate squeezes back, relief spreading over her face.

KATE: Don't let go.
HARRY: I won't.
KATE: Promise.
HARRY: I promise.

KATE: If they get my blood they'll control me.
HARRY: I won't let anyone get your blood, I promise.

> *This starts to ease Kate's mind. Gradually she begins to regain control.*

SCENE 95   INT. HARRY AND KATE'S APARTMENT/ BATHROOM – NIGHT   {63}

Kate sits quietly on the edge of the bath while Harry finishes wrapping her leg. He collects the remaining rags, takes out his Zippo lighter, unscrews the lid and douses them with kerosene. He sets fire to the rags and drops them into the bath. Harry and Kate hug each other and watch as black smoke rises from the bath.

{SCENE 96   EXT. HARRY AND KATE'S BUILDING – DAY

Harry leaves his apartment building. He is about to cross the street when he stops to look. An old black sedan is slowly backing up the street towards him. Harry walks away, throwing worried glances back at the car.

SCENE 97   INT. HARRY AND KATE'S APARTMENT – NIGHT

Kate rolls over, her hand groping for Harry. She opens her eyes and looks around: the bed is empty. Harry sits in a chair staring out the window. Kate crosses to him, wrapped in a blanket.

KATE: Harry?
HARRY: [*without turning*] What are you doing up?
KATE: I always wake up when you're not there. I've been waking up every night for a week.
HARRY: I've got a lot on my mind.

> *Kate leans against the window sill and touches his shoulder.*

KATE: Like what?
HARRY: Get down!

> *He jerks her arm and pulls her roughly to the ground.*

KATE: Ow!

HARRY: Stay away from the window.
KATE: What's out there?

SCENE 98   EXT. HARRY AND KATE'S BUILDING – NIGHT

Through the lace curtains they can see the black sedan parked on the opposite side of the street.

SCENE 99   INT. HARRY AND KATE'S APARTMENT – NIGHT

HARRY: That car's been there every night for the last week.
KATE: What car?
HARRY: The black one.
KATE: That's Joey's car.
HARRY: Who's Joey?
KATE: He lives downstairs. You've met him.
HARRY: How come he has a new car all of a sudden?
KATE: I don't know! He bought it! People are allowed to buy cars, aren't they?

> *Harry rubs his eyes. He slumps down and shakes his head. He seems to become himself again. Kate kneels down and squeezes him tight.*

KATE: I'm scared, Harry.
HARRY: Me too.}

SCENE 100   INT. LAUNDROMAT – DAY   {68}

The Wheel of Fortune spins, stopping on the three-hundred-dollar mark.

JOHN BURGESS: For three hundred dollars ...
CONTESTANT: Give me a 'D'
JOHN BURGESS: We have one 'D'

> *Adriana turns the letter.*

CONTESTANT: I'd like to solve the puzzle.
JOHN BURGESS: Okay ...
CONTESTANT: 'One-way street'.

We pull back from the TV to reveal Kate sitting on a bench making notes, puzzled.

SCENE 101   INT. PERSONNEL OFFICE/HARRY'S CUBICLE –
DAY   {64, 69}

We pan across Sam's clown painting, past a photograph of Kate and another one of Morris, Louise and Sam, past a symmetrical arrangement of perfectly sharpened pencils, stopping on Harry, who is hard at work at his computer. He glances up and notices the Executive Director chatting with his supervisor. They glance over in his direction. Harry looks away and shakes all paranoid thoughts out of his head.

SUPERVISOR: Harry …

> *Harry starts.*

Whoa there, champ; take deep breaths. Mr. Johanson wants to see you.
HARRY: What about?
SUPERVISOR: [*shrugging*] I dunno'.

> *He sees Harry's agitation.*

Remember: take it easy.

SCENE 102   INT. LAUNDROMAT – DAY   {70}

Kate sits brooding over the clue while Wheel of Fortune *plays on.*

CONTESTANT: I'd like to solve the puzzle.
JOHN BURGESS: Okay.
CONTESTANT: 'Worst-case scenario'
KATE: Oh no …

SCENE 102   INT. PERSONNEL OFFICE/BOSS'S OFFICE –
DAY   {71}

Harry sits opposite the Executive Director who gives him a long, sympathetic look.

HARRY: I've done a good job, haven't I?

EXECUTIVE DIRECTOR: I wish you had been honest with me, Harry.

HARRY: If I'd been honest, I wouldn't have this job.

EXECUTIVE DIRECTOR: You put me in an embarrassing position. If something were to happen, and one of the clients were to find out ...

HARRY: Please ... I have to have this job: I have a baby coming.

EXECUTIVE DIRECTOR: I am sorry.

Harry has been here before; he knows it's over. He nods, rises and smiles, trying to hold on to the final strand of his dignity.

HARRY: Don't feel bad.{ I understand.

SCENE 103   INT. PERSONNEL OFFICE/HARRY'S CUBICLE – DAY

Harry approaches his desk and stops. The supervisor is already helping another programmer take over his job.

VOICES: [*hissing*] Harry!}

SCENE 104   INT. PERSONNEL OFFICE/ELEVATOR – DAY{72}

Harry stands at the front of the crowded elevator. The elevator hums and rattles.

{VOICES: [*whispering*] Harry!}

Harry's head spins to the faces around him. They stare at him blankly. Harry turns back, but his eyes flicker back and forth.

{VOICES: [*whispering, with growing derision*] What did you expect? You worthless sack of shit!

Harry stands petrified as the voices hiss and laugh. The elevator doors open and Harry explodes forward.

SCENE 105   INT. PERSONNEL OFFICE/LOBBY – DAY

Harry stands pressed into a corner.

VOICES: Your time's up Harry; it's all over.

> *Derisive laughter follows him as he hurries across the lobby and through the door marked 'MEN'.}*

SCENE 106   INT. PERSONNEL OFFICE/MEN'S ROOM – DAY
{78}

* *Harry sits scrunched up in the corner of a toilet stall. The camera slowly spirals down as the voices grow in volume and number.*

{VOICES: Do it, Harry. Get it over with. You'll be doing everyone a favour.

HARRY: Shut up!

VOICES: Do it! Get it over with, Harry!

> *His name reverberates louder and louder. He covers his ears but it's no use. Outside the cubicle, the entrance door opens and a businessman enters the empty room. He turns on the tap to wash his hands when he hears Harry's stifled screams.*

HARRY: [*out of view*] Aaah!

> *The businessman backs away in fear as Harry tries to shout over the voices screaming in his head*

Please help me.

BUSINESSMAN: You want an ambulance?

HARRY: No, call Kate ...

> *Suddenly we are in Harry's head again and the sound is deafening. Harry writhes and screams. The businessman runs out of the toilet, spooked.}*

SCENE 107   INT. LAUNDROMAT – DAY
{73}

Kate goes to the pay phone, drops in a coin and dials.

KATE: Hi, Harry Goodman, please.

> *Kate waits. {Finally the operator comes back on.*

---

* Note: the filmed scene contains significant differences.

Well, where is he?

> *She listens.*

What do you mean?

> *She listens.*

But he ...

> *As she listens, a shadow creeps across her face. Kate shakes her head, hangs up the phone and hugs herself with growing anxiety.}*

SCENE 108   EXT. HARRY AND KATE'S APARTMENT – NIGHT   {79}

Quick footsteps echo as Morris lumbers into view and beyond.

SCENE 109   INT. HARRY AND KATE'S APARTMENT – NIGHT   {80}

Morris finds the door to Harry and Kate's apartment wide open.

MORRIS: Kate?

> *He waits for an answer then knocks on the door frame. He notices Kate's laundry strewn across the floor.*

Kate, it's Morris.

> *Morris begins to sense that something is wrong. He steps over the sheets strewn in the doorway.*

Kate ...

> *Morris stops as he sees a trail of clothes leading to the corner. Morris looks up and realises that Kate is wedged into the corner by the bed, clutching at a bundle of sheets like a frightened animal.*

Kate?

> *Kate stares into space. Morris picks up the phone and dials.*

SCENE 110   EXT. HARRY AND KATE'S BUILDING – NIGHT
{82}

(Note: in the filmed scene Harry leads the paramedics into the lift in the foyer.) A siren wails as an ambulance appears in the street below. Morris rushes out into the street and leads two paramedics up the stairs.

SCENE 111   INT. HARRY AND KATE'S APARTMENT – NIGHT
{83}

(Note: the filmed scene contains significant differences.) Morris races up followed by the paramedics.

MORRIS: Her doctor's calling back.
FIRST PARAMEDIC: How many months pregnant is she?

> *They rush into the apartment.*

MORRIS: I think about five or six.

> *Morris looks behind the bed but Kate has gone. They look up at the door to the bathroom which is now shut.*

Kate?

> *He goes to the door and tries the handle: it's locked. Morris fears the worst.*

Kate, open the door.

> *The paramedics crowd in behind him.*

FIRST PARAMEDIC: Step aside please.
MORRIS: She's very scared ...
FIRST PARAMEDIC: Please step aside.

> *Morris nods as he backs out of the narrow space.*

Kate, we're here to help you. Please open the door.

> *Without waiting, the second paramedic kneels to examine the lock. He stands back and nods to his partner. They both run at the door, easily breaking the lock.*

SCENE 112   INT. HARRY AND KATE'S APARTMENT/
BATHROOM – NIGHT   {84, 86}

(Note: the filmed scenes contain significant differences.) The door flies open to reveal Kate cowering in the shower stall. The first paramedic approaches, his hands held high, his voice soothing.

FIRST PARAMEDIC: It's okay. {We're not going to hurt you.
KATE: [*screaming in panic*] Don't touch me! [*Crying*] Please, get
   Harry, get Harry ...

> *The second paramedic already has the kit open. He carefully loads the syringe and turns to Morris.*

SECOND PARAMEDIC: She's a bit all over the shop. Could you give
   us a hand?

> *Morris nods.*

> *Morris enters and raises a hand for the paramedic to wait.*

MORRIS: Kate, it's me, Morris. Can I come in?

> *Kate stares at him as he moves closer.*

> *Kate's point of view: a strange mixture of sensory distortions; Morris is out of focus, while the light above his head flares brightly. Shadows creep across the wall.*

It's gunna be okay.}
KATE: Harry?
{MORRIS: I'll find Harry.

> *Kate nods trustingly. The second paramedic moves in, causing her to panic.*

It's gunna' be okay. He's not going to hurt you.

> *Kate doesn't look so sure. He swabs her arm and positions the needle. Kate screams and struggles, the needle snaps off in her arm. Kate bellows.*

SECOND PARAMEDIC: Needle snapped!

Kate clutches herself in pain as blood trickles from the wound. She glares at Morris.

KATE: Thanks a lot.

The paramedic holds her arm and wipes at the blood.

Give me that! Give me that!

The paramedic spreads himself across her, trying to pin her down. Kate struggles hysterically, then stops and stares up at Morris. Morris strokes her hair to calm her down.

MORRIS: [*upset*] I'm sorry Kate. I'm sorry.

The first paramedic hands his partner the new hypodermic. This time the drug goes in smoothly. Kate watches impassively as he takes out the needle and swabs the drop of blood.

KATE: Don't let them take my blood. Harry ... Harry ...

Kate drifts off into a more peaceful place.

Harry ...}

SCENE 113   INT. PSYCHIATRIC HOSPITAL/LOCK-UP WARD – DAY   {85, 87}

Through a glass door the outside door unlocks and Harry's face appears, surrounded by two paramedics, two orderlies and Harry's nurse. The nurse unlocks the second door which opens to reveal Harry is in a wheelchair, passive, hopeless and lost. The paramedics and orderlies are careful to keep him contained. Black out.

SCENE 114   INT. PSYCHIATRIC HOSPITAL/ROOM – DAY{88}

(Note: the filmed scene contains significant differences.) Get-well cards and homemade gifts from the clubhouse line Harry's dressing table.

{DR NORBERG: Rowan and Frank have been asking after you. Also, Dave says he's forgiven you.

Harry smiles, a half-eaten lunch tray in front of him. Dr Norberg sits beside him.

HARRY: Can I see her?
DR NORBERG: Perhaps it's a good idea to wait.
HARRY: You don't understand. She needs me.}
DR NORBERG: Harry, Kate doesn't want to see you.
{NURSE: Finished?
HARRY: Yeah thank you. It was horrible.

> *A nurse glances down at his tray and frowns.*

NURSE: Harry ...
HARRY: Whoops.}

> *He takes a miniature paper cup from the tray, throws the pills down his throat and washes them down. {He opens his mouth wide and pokes out his tongue.*

HARRY: All gone, see?

> *The nurse moves to another patient.*

[*To Dr Norberg*] I don't believe you.}

SCENE 115   EXT. MORRIS' HOUSE – DAY   {89}

Autumn leaves blow across the concrete driveway as Morris' station wagon pulls in.

SCENE 116   INT. MORRIS' HOUSE/HARRY'S ROOM – DAY
                                                  {90}

Morris opens the door and steps in, trying to be as cheerful as he can. Harry puts his bag on the bed and looks around. There are some neatly stacked packing cartons in the corner.

MORRIS: It's just like you left it.

> *Morris retreats, leaving Harry alone. He looks around his old room: right back to square one. He crosses to the packing cartons, opens the top one, and pulls out Kate's home-made quilt.*

SCENE 117   INT. MORRIS' HOUSE/BATHROOM – DAY   {94}

He crosses to the lists pinned on the wall, a reminder of a previous life.

{He opens the cabinet, stares at his medication, then slams it shut.}

SCENE 118   INT. CLUBHOUSE/MEETING AREA – DAY   {96}

Wheel of Fortune *plays on the TV. Rowan and Dave sit bickering over Rowan's black-and-white TV. We move across to Harry who sits beside the mumbling Frank, making notes in Kate's special book. The big wheel spins ...*

*{*SCENE 119   EXT. STREET/APPLIANCE STORE – DAY

Harry makes notes, standing outside the appliance store where he first took Kate ... The TV plays Wheel Of Fortune.

SCENE 120   EXT. WON KOK RESTAURANT – DAY

Harry stands outside the restaurant. He looks around, then focuses on a derelict building across the road.}

SCENE 121   EXT. EMPTY BUILDING – DAY   {100}

He crosses the street, checks that the coast is clear, then pulls at some loose boards and enters the building.

SCENE 122   INT. MORRIS' HOUSE – DAY   {97}

Sam kneels on the carpet beside Morris, who is lying on his side, {groaning, his arm disappeared into the heating duct up to his shoulder}. Sam looks up as Harry enters and heads towards the door.

SAM: Uncle Harry, where's Kate?
MORRIS: Sam ...
HARRY: I think I'll go for a walk.

     Morris struggles to get up.

MORRIS: You want some company?
HARRY: [*firm*] Thanks. I prefer to be alone right now.

SCENE 123   INT. BUS – DAY   {93}

Harry {moves through the empty bus and} sits {down. The bus is empty, except for three old women dressed in black sitting opposite him: the youngest is busy twisting thread from a ball of yarn. The middle one measures the thread at arm's length and the third older woman snips the thread off with a pair of scissors. The women whisper & cluck between themselves.}

SCENE 124 INT. PSYCHIATRIC HOSPITAL/ENTRANCE – DAY {91}

The entrance door buzzes open as an orderly escorts Harry through the security door with a wire-reinforced observation window.

SCENE 125 INT. PSYCHIATRIC HOSPITAL/SAFETY LOCK – DAY {92 ❊}

{*The orderly stops at the table and waits. Harry hands him his plastic carry bag and watches while he searches through it. Satisfied,*} *the orderly unlocks the next door with a key from a ring hung on his belt.*

SCENE 126 INT. PSYCHIATRIC HOSPITAL/WARD – DAY {92 ❊, 98 ❊}

A nurse leads us down the row of beds filled with women in various states of mental decay: paranoid stares, facial twitches, rolling tongues, compulsive clawing. Harry looks around him. The idea that Kate has to deal with this every day is enough to break Harry's heart.

NURSE: [*loudly*] Kate, you have a visitor.

> *Harry almost doesn't recognise her. Her eyes are sunken, her hair is matted and, worst of all, someone has tried to spruce her up with some blue eye-shadow and rouge. The nurse grins at him, wearing the same colour eye-shadow.*

Doesn't she look cute?

> *Someone starts shouting in a distant room. The nurse goes back up the ward, leaving Harry and Kate alone.*

HARRY: Kate ...

She looks up at him with heavily medicated eyes. He takes a tissue, licks it and tries to wipe the make-up off her face.

I'm going to get you out of here.

KATE: [*dreamy*] I'm tired, Harry. I want to go up there.

HARRY: You can't leave me.

KATE: Come with me, Harry; it'll be so beautiful.

HARRY: What about Astral?

KATE: She's there, waiting for us.

HARRY: No, you're wrong. She's here ...

He puts his hand on her stomach.

KATE: What if we are crazy?

Harry is shocked that she could even suggest it.

HARRY: I've been watching the *Wheel*. Look, the bonus rounds are written in red.

She glances at the book. Harry knows he's made contact. {The nurse and another orderly stop in the doorway. Their point of view: Harry sits beside Kate holding her hand.

ORDERLY: [*sotto voce*] Who's that?

NURSE: Her boy friend.}

Harry places the notebook in her hands.

HARRY: Look at the first one: 'Necessity is the mother of invention'. I think that's pretty self-explanatory, but look at the next one: it's an artist and title; Maurice Chevalier 'Thank Heaven For Little Girls'.

Harry waits for her to react. She looks up, a glimmer of her old spark reappears in her eyes.

Okay, I know what you're thinking: how do we get you out of here? Where can we go? The final clue: A phrase, 'Run and hide'.

{KATE: I love you.

Harry almost starts to cry, he is so happy.

HARRY: I love you too. I'm getting you out of here right now. Okay?

> *Kate nods. He crosses around the bed to Kate's chest of drawers, kneels down and pulls out her street clothes. Keeping them hidden from sight, Harry moves back to his seat, glancing towards the door. He sees the nurse wheel a cart past the door, pausing to smile as she goes. Harry waits a moment, then quickly pulls down Kate's bedclothes and helps her swing her legs out of bed.}*

SCENE 127   INT. PSYCHIATRIC HOSPITAL/BATHROOM – DAY   {98 ✳}

{Harry leads Kate into the bathroom. She is slow and weak from the high doses of medication so he helps her sit down on the closed toilet.} He unties her hospital gown and eases up her arms.

{HARRY: Arms up.}

> *Kate raises her arms. Harry hastily pulls the dress over her head, {then helps her to her feet. He takes a headband and gathers her hair, then pulls a baseball cap low over her forehead.}*

{SCENE 128   INT. PSYCHIATRIC HOSPITAL/WARD – DAY

Harry and Kate emerge from the bathroom and move through the ward towards the corridor. The other clients are so heavily medicated, they barely register what's happening.}

SCENE 129   INT. PSYCHIATRIC HOSPITAL/CORRIDOR – DAY   {98 ✳}

(Note: the filmed scene contains significant differences.) {The camera follows Harry's shoes and Kate's slippers, then moves up to reveal Harry supporting Kate, who is now wearing sunglasses.

KATE: They'll see my feet.
HARRY: They're not looking at your feet.}

Down the end of the corridor, the orderlies are letting other visitors out. As they get closer, Kate clings tighter to Harry's arm. Harry grabs an elderly woman wearing a hospital gown.

Grandma, there you are! We've been looking for you.

Harry puts 'Grandma' under his other arm and they move towards the door as if she were seeing them off.

Now take care of yourself and do what the doctors tell you.
GRANDMA: Do I know you?

They walk past Kate's nurse who is so busy with other clients and visitors that she doesn't look twice. Finally, they reach the security door. The orderly holds it open impatiently.

HARRY: Bye, Grandma; we'll see you next week.

Harry and Kate both kiss Grandma goodbye. She waves as Kate disappears through the door.

GRANDMA: Bye ...

Just then Kate's nurse emerges from another ward and catches sight of Harry. She smiles. Harry smiles back but his tension shows through. The nurse still thinks nothing of it and heads back towards the women's ward.

{SCENE 130   INT. PSYCHIATRIC HOSPITAL/SECURITY LOCK – DAY

The orderly locks the door after them, then unlocks the second door. Harry smiles.

HARRY: See ya next week.

SCENE 131   INT. PSYCHIATRIC HOSPITAL/LOBBY – DAY

Harry presses the button and they stand waiting for the elevator. The floor number reads, '8'. Another visitor stands next to them. Harry pushes the button again. The elevator bell dings. The doors open to reveal two orderlies. Harry and Kate don't have a choice. They enter, Harry smiling around him.}

SCENE 132   INT. PSYCHIATRIC HOSPITAL/ELEVATOR – DAY   {98 ✿}

The pressure is starting to show on Harry's face. The two orderlies look at Harry and Kate impassively.

SCENE 133   INT. PSYCHIATRIC HOSPITAL/ENTRANCE – DAY   {98 ✿}

Harry and Kate emerge from the elevator while the two orderlies go the other way. They begin the walk towards the glass doors. A security guard sits at his desk. The phone rings. He picks up the phone and listens. Harry and Kate keep moving, finally reaching the doors. Harry glances back, then rushes to get Kate out.

SCENE 134   EXT. PSYCHIATRIC HOSPITAL – DAY   {99}

Harry tries to move Kate as quickly as he can. She can barely keep her balance as they step off the curb and onto the busy six-lane highway. {The traffic is thick and fast. They narrowly miss being swiped by a passing van. Kate freezes and has to be dragged forward as Harry moves them through the honking traffic.

SCENE 135   INT. WON KWOK RESTAURANT – NIGHT

Harry rubs clean an item on the specials board even though the two tables in the corner are deserted. Mr Chin drops two large take-away orders on the counter before him and explains to Harry where they have to be delivered.

SCENE 136   EXT. WON KWOK RESTAURANT – NIGHT

Harry secures the boxes on the back of a bicycle, then pushes off.}

SCENE 137   INT. EMPTY BUILDING – DAY   {101}

Harry has set up a mattress, a camping burner, a bucket and a few other primitive amenities. Kate sits on a crate, noticeably pregnant, her feet in a shallow plastic tub. She watches impassively, while Harry kneels before her, washing her feet and calves.

SCENE 138   INT. EMPTY BUILDING – DAY   {103}

{*Kate finishes stuffing a spring roll into her mouth, then without pausing picks up another one. She stuffs her face with olives, potato chips and chocolate.*} *Harry and Kate exercise, striding around the perimeter of the room.* {*Harry collapses on the ground. Kate stops and tries to pull him up. He pulls her down and they roll on the floor, Kate pulling at his clothes.*}

SCENE 139   EXT. CLUBHOUSE – DAY   {104 ✲}

Dave, Rowan and Frank emerge from the entrance and cross the street, passing by the parking structure opposite.

{ROWAN: You owe me fifty cents.
DAVE: When?}
ROWAN: Last week!
DAVE: Rowan, you're hallucinating again.
ROWAN: I am not!

    Harry steps out from the shadows.

HARRY: Hey! Dave! Rowan!

SCENE 140   INT. PARKING STRUCTURE OPPOSITE CLUBHOUSE – DAY   {104 ✲}

Frank stands looking out while Rowan shakes his head vigorously.

HARRY: Please Rowan ...
ROWAN: Not my TV ...
DAVE: [*shoving him*] Give it to him, ya moron.

SCENE 141   INT. EMPTY BUILDING – DAY   {105}

Chinese food cartons cover the mattress and surrounding floor. Kate sits propped up on the mattress, eating a tub of ice-cream. She is surrounded by cartons, chocolate bars, and other essentials for surviving a pregnancy. Harry is busy setting up Rowan's TV set.

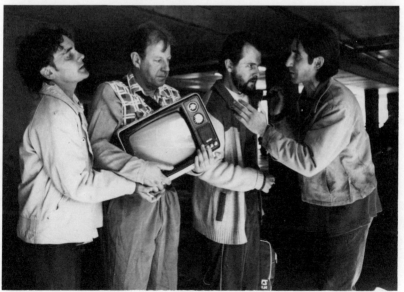

KATE: Hurry up, it's about to start. [*Mouth full*] This is fabulous.

Harry grins to himself, happy to have the old Kate back.

KATE: [*slightly urgent*] Harry ...

The spoon drops and clatters on the concrete. Harry trips over himself getting across to the bed.

HARRY: What? What is it?

Kate takes his hand and places it on her swollen stomach. They grin in amazement.

KATE: She's trying to tell us something.
HARRY: [*listening*] Yes, I can hear it. 'N' ... 'O', new word, 'M' ... 'O' ... 'R' ... 'E' ... 'No more ice cream'.

Kate pulls him down beside her on the bed. They kiss and cuddle in complete bliss.

KATE: Turn on the TV.

Harry stands and goes to the old black-and-white set.

HARRY: So what are you going to ask today?
KATE: I just want to check that she's okay. We'll need to save up for the big questions.

Harry flicks around the channels. He checks his watch. Kate struggles to her feet and crosses to sit beside Harry.

KATE: Where's *Wheel of Fortune*?
HARRY: I don't know.
KATE: This isn't good.
HARRY: It's probably just a programming thing.

Kate is starting to get anxious.

KATE: It's a bad sign, I know it is.
HARRY: It's not a bad sign. I'll go and call the station. I'll be right back, okay?
KATE: I want to come with you.
HARRY: Kate, I'll be right back.

{*Kate doesn't look reassured. Harry realises she is not going to calm down. He reaches into his pocket, searches around and pulls out ... a piece of chalk.*

This'll protect you ...

Kate watches as he squats and traces a thick line of chalk around the bed.

Just stay inside this circle and you'll be safe. Okay?

Kate nods and watches as} *Harry disappears into the shadows, his footsteps echoing.*

SCENE 142   EXT. STREET/PHONE BOOTH – DUSK   {106}

HARRY: [*into phone*] Yeah, but it's usually ...

He listens.

For how long?

He glances around nervously.

There's no way you can get them to go on holidays later ... ?

He listens.

You don't understand how important it is ...

He listens, then hangs up the phone.

{SCENE 143   INT. EMPTY BUILDING – DAY

Kate stares in disbelief.

KATE: Holidays ... ?
HARRY: It's only for six weeks ...

Harry steps towards her but she pushes him away.

KATE: Six weeks!
HARRY: It's not that long.
KATE: I'm due in four weeks! Oh, Harry, I think we're in trouble.
HARRY: Don't say that.

KATE: I think we're in big trouble.

Harry grabs her by the shoulders and looks her straight in the eye.

HARRY: Kate, listen, I'm going to get some help.
KATE: What do you mean?
HARRY: I don't know. Just hold on, okay?
KATE: [*nodding*] Okay ...

Being careful not to hurt the baby, they hug each other tightly.}

SCENE 144   INT. MORRIS' HOUSE/LIVING ROOM – DAY
{107}

We pan across the empty room as there is a crashing and rummaging from one of the bedrooms. We stop on the window where Morris' station wagon pulls up the driveway. The door unlocks and Sam runs in, nearly stumbling as he helps Morris carry in the groceries.

MORRIS: Sam, don't run ...

Morris stops as he hears a loud crashing of objects from inside the house.

HARRY [*off screen*] It's okay! It's just me!
SAM: Harry!

He runs excitedly towards the voice, leaving Morris to drop his groceries and follow.

SCENE 145   INT. MORRIS' HOUSE/HARRY'S ROOM – DAY
{108}

Harry is giving Sam a big hug and a kiss when Morris appears in the door. Morris looks around the room, which is piled with the contents of the boxes from Harry and Kate's apartment. Harry sees Morris' expression and allows Sam to slide to the ground.

MORRIS: We've been worried sick about you.
HARRY: I'm okay.
MORRIS: You understand what kind of danger you're putting Kate in.

Sam is fossicking around the mess, having a great time.

Sam, go outside.

SAM: I'm helping!

MORRIS: Go outside!

Sam is surprised by his father's tone and makes a quick exit. Morris takes a breath, softening his anger.

MORRIS: I'm sorry, Harry, I can't do this any more. I know I'm being selfish, but fuck it: I want my life back.

HARRY: Kate's in bad shape, Morrie. She needs medication really bad.

MORRIS: She should be in a hospital.

HARRY: Don't you understand? They're after us. They cut off our pension. They want to take away our baby.

Morris realises that Harry is not in control. He looks around at the mess.

MORRIS: What are you doing here?

Harry reads his expression, becomes self-conscious and immediately calms down.

HARRY: I was looking for Kate's prescriptions.

MORRIS: They're in my office.

Morris thinks about it and shakes his head as if he can't believe he's doing this.

Okay, I'll bring you Kate's medication, but if I think Kate needs to go to hospital, then we take her.

HARRY: I can't make deals for Kate.

MORRIS: [*turning*] Then forget it.

HARRY: Morrie, okay!

Morris shakes his head at himself.

SCENE 146   EXT. EMPTY BUILDING – NIGHT   {109}

Harry paces the edge of the gutter back and forth. He checks his watch. Headlights drive towards him; he waves as Morris' station wagon pulls up. Harry opens the back door and starts unstrapping Sam. Morris comes around and lifts Sam, who is fast asleep, into his arms.

MORRIS: I couldn't find a baby sitter.

SCENE 147   INT. EMPTY BUILDING/STAIRWELL – NIGHT
{110✿}

Two torch beams move up the stairs as Harry and Morris round the corner, Morris puffing under the weight of Sam. Morris moves ahead as Harry stops to secure the door. Suddenly, Dave leaps out into the beam of Morris' light.

DAVE: Who goes there!

> *Morris drops the torch, letting out an involuntary shout.*

MORRIS: Shit ...

> *Sam wakes and gives a sleepy groan. Harry has moved up the stairs.*

HARRY: Dave, it's just me and Morrie. You remember Morrie.
MORRIS: [*feeling tense himself*] Hi, Dave.

> *Dave glares at him suspiciously.*

DAVE: I'm keeping watch.
HARRY: And you're doing an incredible job.

> *Morris gives Harry a filthy look as they move on.*

SCENE 148   INT. EMPTY BUILDING – NIGHT   {110✿}

Rowan sits on a chair, his hands gripping the edges of the seat. Frank stands behind Rowan, mumbling to himself. Kate sits on her mattress in the chalk circle, sweating, making a great effort to stay calm. Harry kneels and kisses Kate, stroking her hair.

KATE: Thanks for coming.
MORRIS: You okay?

> *Kate nods her head without much conviction. Morris gives*

Rowan and Frank a worried look and pulls a prescription bottle out of his pocket.

I brought you something.

Kate almost gasps with relief. She squeezes Harry's arm in anticipation as Morris pulls open the bottle, cracks the seal and hands it to her. Rowan watches hungrily.

Want some wa – ?

Kate has thrown the pills down in a single gulp. The security of the medication has already calmed her.

KATE: Better already, see?

Sam is now awake.

SAM: I have to go to the toilet.

Harry and Kate laugh out loud, loving the atmosphere of normality a child brings.

KATE: [*struggling to rise*] I'll take you.
HARRY: You sure ... ?
KATE: [*pushing his hand away*] It's good for the baby. C'mon, Sam ...

Morris smiles, keeping a watchful eye. Kate winces as she grabs her lower stomach. Morris looks concerned as Harry helps her to stand. She takes Sam's hand, supports her back with her other hand and waddles across the floor towards the bathroom. Morris waits until she shuts the door.

MORRIS: I don't know ... How are you going to get her to the hospital?
HARRY: I'll call a taxi.
MORRIS: It's so ... dirty in here.

Harry smiles at his brother's fussiness, emotion welling. Spontaneously, he hugs Morris. They break off and smile, feeling closer again. Suddenly Kate screams, lacerating the silence. Dave runs in, wild-eyed shouting. Rowan's eyes flicker around in panic. Harry and Morris sprint towards the bathroom as Frank mumbles louder and faster.

SCENE 149   INT. EMPTY BUILDING/BATHROOM – NIGHT

{110 ✳}

Sam stands staring. Harry and Morris burst into the gutted toilet. They stop, shocked at what they see.

Kate is sitting on the floor in complete shock, surrounded by her own blood. Morris lunges at Sam, sweeping him into his arms, hiding his face. Harry and Morris look at each other for a moment in complete helplessness.

HARRY: Call an ambulance.

> *Morris nods and rushes out, still carrying Sam, past Dave, Rowan and Frank who are crowding in the doorway. Harry blocks their way and shepherds them back out the door.*

Come on guys, get out.
ROWAN: What's the matter with Kate?
HARRY: Just get out! Go!

> *They nod, completely disconnected from what's happening, turn and move out. Harry turns back to Kate and has to look away again, his anguish is so intense.*

KATE: Harry ... ?

He pulls himself together and turns, crosses around and kneels beside Kate. She stares in front of her clutching at her dress trying mechanically to stop the flow of blood from between her legs. Harry wraps his arms around her and hugs her tight. A guttural animal groan comes from somewhere deep inside her and repeats itself. Harry tries to respond with a cooing sound, soothing but also very primal. They rock together, waiting for the ambulance.

SCENE 150   INT. HOSPITAL/CORRIDOR – NIGHT   {111}

Kate lies on the gurney as it races down the corridor. Above her head the fluorescent lights strobe. Kate is wheeled into the operating theatre, her eyes wild with fear.

SCENE 151   INT. HOSPITAL/EMERGENCY RECEPTION –
NIGHT   {112}

(Note: the filmed scene contains significant differences.) Louise tucks a coat over Sam who is asleep across the orange vinyl chairs. She moves across to Morris and Harry who are waiting by the doors.

LOUISE: [*sotto*] Can you understand how scared that little boy is?

Morris opens his mouth to speak.

Don't you say *anything*. You! You have no excuse.

They are interrupted by the staff obstetrician, in her thirties. She comes through the swinging doors with a sense of urgency.

OBSTETRICIAN: Who's her obstetrician?

Morris and Louise look down at their shoes.

HARRY: She doesn't have one.

OBSTETRICIAN: Does she take any medication?

HARRY: Ah, just Stelazine and um ... Benztropine.

OBSTETRICIAN: Any allergies? Any problems with anaesthetics?

HARRY: I don't know. She going to be okay?

OBSTETRICIAN: We've stopped the bleeding but the baby needs to be delivered urgently. The safest way is a caesarean.

HARRY: No knives.

OBSTETRICIAN: That's what she said. What's going on?

Morris and Louise exchange looks; they're not going to persuade Harry to give his consent.

LOUISE: Is there an alternative?

OBSTETRICIAN: We could induce labour, but there's a risk the bleeding could start up again.

{HARRY: Shut up! You heard me!

The obstetrician is stunned. Louise and Morris look puzzled, then realise Harry is responding to his voices.

MORRIS: [*closing his eyes*] Jesus Christ.

Deafening screams: suddenly we're inside Harry's head and it's a wonder he can even speak.

HARRY: Aaah. Wait! [*Pointing at the obstetrician*] Wait for me!

> *He runs towards the bathroom.*

SCENE 152   INT. HOSPITAL/BATHROOM – NIGHT

Water gushes as Harry's hand twists the water full on. His voices laugh.

VOICES: Forget it, Harry. It's all over, and there's nothing you can
  do. Harry! Harry, did you see the blood?
HARRY: Shut the fuck up!
VOICES: Oooh! We're *sooo* scared! The blood was baaad ...

> *The voices laugh and laugh. Harry takes a deep breath, clenches
> his teeth.*

SCENE 153   INT. HOSPITAL/WAITING ROOM – NIGHT

*Morris is busy signing release forms while the obstetrician explains.
Meanwhile, Louise, who is carrying a sleeping Sam, kisses Morris and
heads towards the door.*

LOUISE: Call me.
OBSTETRICIAN: This release basically says that I advised a
  caesarean ...

> *She falls silent as Harry walks into the room, clutching his hands
> protectively; he seems to have the voices under control. His brow
> is taut with tension.*

MORRIS: Harry ... ?
HARRY: Doctor, I'd like to see her.

> *The obstetrician looks at him uncertainly.*

  I can help her.

SCENE 154   INT. HOSPITAL/DELIVERY ROOM – NIGHT

Kate lies, scared, her breathing shallow.

KATE: Oh God, oh God, oh God ...

As the pain subsides she starts to weep.

Harry.

The doors swing open and the obstetrician enters, revealing Harry outside, struggling to put on some surgical garments.

SCENE 155   INT. HOSPITAL/CORRIDOR – NIGHT

Morris helps Harry put on the garments and mask. Morris sees Harry's hands are shaking.

HARRY: I'll be okay.

SCENE 156   INT. HOSPITAL/DELIVERY ROOM – NIGHT

Monitoring equipment flickers with digital read-outs and graphic lines to show the baby's vital signs. Harry crouches beside Kate and wipes her brow. She is so relieved she tries to embrace him, causing herself another convulsion of pain. Harry pushes her down and leans over so they can embrace.

KATE: Where the hell have you been?

Harry smiles, and hushes her as the obstetrician approaches.

OBSTETRICIAN: Okay, Kate, we're going to give you some pethedine to help with the contractions.

Kate looks at Harry for a decision. Harry nods so she nods in agreement. Kate braces herself as the nurse disappears behind the mound of her belly with a needle.

OBSTETRICIAN: Take a deep breath and hold on.

Kate takes a deep breath and gasps in pain. Harry's eyes widen in panic.

And again.
KATE: Again?

The obstetrician nods. This time she lets out a scream you could hear in the parking lot.}

SCENE 157   INT. HOSPITAL/DELIVERY ROOM – NIGHT{113}

Kate sweats and strains while Harry sits beside her, fretting.*

OBSTETRICIAN: The baby's ready.

> *The monitors continue to beep and flicker in a constant rhythm. The nurses look at each other in relief. Harry kisses Kate on the forehead.*

KATE: What did she say?
HARRY: She said the baby's ready.

> *The obstetrician freezes, looking down between her legs. The monitors jump and flatten out as the digital numbers go haywire. The nurse looks up at the obstetrician. Harry sees the expression on their faces.*

HARRY: What's happening?

> *They don't react. Kate struggles to sit up which brings the obstetrician's attention back into focus.*

OBSTETRICIAN: Kate, I need you to roll onto your side.
HARRY: What's happening?

> *The obstetrician gives him a cold glance. Now Kate is aware that something is wrong.*

KATE: What's the matter?

> *Harry can't answer; he's in shock. Kate grimaces and struggles to sit up.*

OBSTETRICIAN: [*with authority*] Kate, please ...

> *Kate isn't listening. Harry squeezes her hand.*

Kate, you're not listening. You have to push really hard because the baby's not liking these contractions much. Mister Goodman ...

> *Kate clutches at Harry like a helpless child.*

---

* Note: the filmed scene contains significant differences.

KATE: Harry ...

Harry pulls himself together. He tries to smile but his face is a deathly grimace.

HARRY: Come on, please. You have to push.

KATE: I can't ...

She starts to struggle, rolling her head back and forth.

HARRY: [*stroking Kate's hair*] I love you Kate.

Harry withers as Kate lets out a terrible scream.

OBSTETRICIAN: [*to a nurse*] Clamp the cord.

The obstetrician moves away from Kate, apparently holding the baby. {The surrounding commotion fades into the background as Harry stares down at Kate.

HARRY: Kate, can you hear me? Kate, she's here, she's still here.

Kate is close to exhaustion; she nods imperceptibly.

Come on, Kate: just this one more time. Focus with me, focus, focus, focus ...

Meanwhile, the obstetrician and nurses are scrambling to revive the baby. The monitors remain flat. Harry closes his eyes and presses his forehead against Kate.

Astral, please. We're ready for you, we are. Astral come, Astral come.

Kate is too winded to speak but she starts to mouth the words. One of the nurses looks up, disturbed by their behaviour. Now they are chanting together, focusing, focusing. The overhead lights fluctuate. The obstetrician and nurses glance up. There is a faint splutter and whimper from the baby. The obstetrician's eyes register surprise.

OBSTETRICIAN: Is the nursery expecting us?

NURSE: Yes doctor.

OBSTETRICIAN: Apgar scores of two at one, and five at five.}

Harry stares around him in amazement as the thin wail of a baby is heard. Kate blinks and tries to focus.

KATE: [*faintly*] She's here? She's really here?

Harry grins and nods, kissing her on the mouth. Harry watches the baby, fascinated. Kate relaxes and smiles. But her eyes defocus completely as her mouth slackens. Slow motion: The obstetrician and nurses huddle around Astral. We get a glimpse of the tiny child, still shiny with blood. Harry turns back to Kate. His smile fades as he looks at Kate. He glances down to her feet, alarm registering on his face as blood splatters over the white linoleum. The obstetrician turns in surprise. She immediately goes into action, shouting orders to the nurses. The first nurse rushes around to Kate's side. The second nurse rushes to the wall phone and calls for emergency. The third nurse resets the equipment. Harry is jostled out of the way by the first nurse. He stares around him, frozen in shock. A thin sheet of blood completely obscures the white linoleum.

{SCENE 158   INT. HOSPITAL/CORRIDOR – NIGHT

As the first nurse shepherds Harry out the door an orderly moves him out of the way as an emergency team wheels in an array of equipment. Morris and Louise, down the hall, see Harry amidst the commotion. They move towards Harry with concern. Harry looks from Morris and Louise back towards the delivery room. They see Harry's fear-stricken face, as the doors swing shut.}

Fade to white. Slow motion ends.

SCENE 159   INT. HOSPITAL/WAITING ROOM – NIGHT
{114 ✿}

Tilt down from the white wall to Harry, staring into space. Morris sits a few seats away, comforting Louise who is the only one of the three crying. Morris glances at Harry, swallowing his emotions. Harry blinks, still unable to feel anything.

OBSTETRICIAN: [*off screen*] Mister Goodman?

Harry looks up in a daze. The obstetrician is standing before him; she looks heart-broken to have lost her patient.

You can see your baby now.

SCENE 160   INT. HOSPITAL/CORRIDOR – NIGHT   {114✹}

A gurney shrouded in white floats down the brightly lit white corridor.

SCENE 161   INT. HOSPITAL/VIEWING BAY – NIGHT   {114✹}

Harry enters and looks into the bright sterile room. Morris appears behind Harry with the obstetrician. Harry presses his face against the glass and stares down in amazement. Astral, a tiny, red-faced thing, squirms in the bright light. Harry moves away from the glass and turns to Morris.

HARRY: I need some air. [*Slowly*] Will you stay here with Astral?

Morris looks at Harry: no answer is necessary. Morris hugs Harry, squeezing him tight. Harry gives them a brave smile and walks out the door.

{SCENE 162   EXT. HOSPITAL – SUNRISE

Harry emerges from the hospital entrance into the still blue morning.

SCENE 163   EXT. STREET – SUNRISE

Harry walks down the empty street.}

SCENE 164   EXT. BRIDGE – SUNRISE   {115}

A lone truck rumbles by as Harry moves onto the bridge. He stares down, then climbs up on the railing. Rain drops patter on the water below. Boom up from behind Harry, arching over his head, down on the vast distance between Harry and the water. We continue around to close on Harry as the rain starts to fall. He tilts back his head and opens his mouth to catch a few drops of moisture.

KATE: [*off screen*] Now I know what peace is, I don't want to stay here without you.

Harry turns. Kate is standing beside him. She starts to flap her arms. Harry joins her and they squawk together.

{*Harry stands on the railing, alone, silhouetted against the blue-grey sky. Suddenly, a semi-trailer roars by, obscuring our view. When the view clears, the railing is empty.***}**

Fade to black.

{SCENE 165   INT. MORRIS' HOUSE/HARRY'S BEDROOM – DAY

Astral's point of view: Sam looks down smiling into the crib.

SAM: Astral, I got something for you. See …

Sam pulls out a piece of the chalk Harry gave him, sticks it in Astral's face, then disappears from view. We hear the sound of scraping chalk. Then Sam reappears.

You're going to live with us now, so I'm going to use it to keep the monsters away.

Sam leans forward and kisses Astral, then disappears. Astral is a very cute little girl several weeks old. She has no idea what's going on.

*Fade out.***}**

THE END

Film End Credits

CAST CREDITS: Harry JOHN LYNCH / Kate JACQUELINE McKENZIE / Morris Goodman COLIN FRIELS / Louise Goodman DEBORRA-LEE FURNESS / Sam Goodman DANIEL DAPERIS / Dr Norberg ROBYN NEVIN / Dave DAVID ARGUE / Rowan GEOFF BROOKS / Frank HUMPHREY BOWER / Obstetrician JANE MENELAUS / Dr Singani ALEX PINDER / Personnel Director MARCUS EYRE / Housing Agent HEATHER BOLTON / Check-Out Cashier SAM JOHNSON / Rose LESLEY BAKER / Lane Manager PETER SARDI / Clubhouse 'Clients' GLYNIS ANGELL SALLY-ANNE UPTON LOIS COLLINDER GUMPY PHILLIPS ALEXIS ANTHOPOULOS JOHN BRUMPTON NEVILLE STONEHOUSE / Paramedics ROBERT MORGAN SIMON WILTON / Psych Nurse LOUISE WATSON / Theatre Nurses BERNADETTE DOYLE STEPHANIE CHEN BERNADETTE RYAN / Rollerblader MARCUS MACRIS / Psych Orderlies PAUL MODER NEIL FOLEY CHRISTOPHER CONNELLY / Psych Security PETER CULPAN / Office Supervisor DINO MARNIKA / Astral ELISE MAYBERRY / Anaesthetist JOHN ZULA / Norberg's Assistant JOHN SCOTT / Elderly Patient ESME MELVILLE / Lift Orderlies GARY ADAMS BEN ROGAN / K-Mart Shopper PEGGY NICHOLLS / Midwife KAREN WESCOMBE / K-Mart Manager VIVIENNE JARDINE / "WHEEL OF FORTUNE" / JOHN BURGESS as himself / ADRIANA XENIDES as herself / and JOHN DEEKS / Contestants CHRISTINE BRETONES PHOEBE DUNN JAYNE JUPP PAULA CARTER RICHARD DURRANT SHAUN McCLELLAND MARILYN COLEMAN KERRY ELLIOTT GREG PARKER KEITH CORNELISSAN PAMELA GARRICK SUZIE STEEN SUSAN CORRELL MANDY JOLLY STEVEN TURNER. **CREW CREDITS:** Producers TIMOTHY WHITE JONATHAN SHTEINMAN / Director & Writer MICHAEL RYMER / Script Editor LOUIS NOWRA / Production Manager YVONNE COLLINS / Production Coordinator JO FRIESEN / Production Accountant BERNADETTE BREITKREUZ / Accounts Assistant CHRIS BLACK / Post Production Coordinator JUDITH HUGHES / Production Runners EMMA JAMVOLD

ROBERT HALL / Director's Attachment   TANJA GEORGE / First
Assistant Director   EUAN KEDDIE / Second Assistant Director
ROBBIE VISSER   / Third Assistant Director   DAMIEN GRANT /
Script Supervisor   JO WEEKS / Location Manager   STEVE BRETT /
Assistant Location Manager   MELISSA RYMER / Unit Managers
ANDY PAPPAS   GENE VAN DAM / Unit Assistant   SEAN
TENNANT / Director of Photography   ELLERY RYAN, ACS /
Camera Operator   ROBERT MURRAY / Focus Puller   SION
MICHEL / Clapper Loader   ANDREW JERRAM / Stills   JENNIFER
MITCHELL / Film Editor   DANY COOPER / Sound Recordist
JOHN PHILLIPS / Boom Operator   STEPHEN VAUGHAN /
Assistant Editor   ANTONY GRAY / Sound Design   FRANK
LIPSON, MPSE / Dialogue Editor   STEVE LAMBETH / Foley
STEVE BURGESS   GERRY LONG / Assistant Sound Editor   ROSS
CHAMBERS / Assistant Sound Mixer   DANNY GADD / Sound Mixer
STEVE BURGESS / Production Designer   CHRIS KENNEDY / Art
Director   HUGH BATEUP / Art Department Coordinator   SHARON
YOUNG / Props Buyer   MARITA MUSSETT / Set Dresser   GLEN
JOHNSON / Standby Props   DEAN SULLIVAN / Art Department
Attachment   JOANNA PARK / Special Effects   CONRAD
ROTHMAN   BRIAN PEARCE / Construction Manager MARTIN
KELLOCK / Foreman   ROBIN HARTLEY / Carpenters   COLIN
GEARMAN   FRANK SAVAGE / Set Painters   GUS LOBB / CLIVE
YOUNG / Scenic Artist   GRAHAM GALLOWAY / Labourer
MARK BYFORD / Costume Designer   KERRI MAZZOCCO /
Standby Wardrobe   ISOBEL CARTER / Assistant Costume
MARTINE SIMMONDS / Makeup Artist   KIRSTEN VEYSEY /
Hairdresser   ZELJKA STANIN / Key Grip   BARRY HANSEN / Grip
NOEL MUDIE / 3rd Grip   JOL SIMPSON / Gaffer   TED
NORDSVAN / Best Boy   JOHN BRENNAN / Generator Operator
GREG DE MARIGNY / Casting   ALISON BARRETT   GREGG
APPS / Casting Assistant   TRISH McASKILL   ALISON BARRETT
CASTING / Extras Casting   MEL GOGGINS   PROTOTYPE / UK
Casting   SUZANNE CROWLEY   GILLY POOLE / Unit Publicity
FIONA SEARSON   DENNIS DAVIDSON ASSOCIATES / Cutting
Rooms   THE FACILITY / Rushes Screenings   DIGITAL FILM
LABORATORIES / Sound Transfers   EUGENE WILSON / Rushes
Syncing   MARIA KALTENTHALER / Telecine Transfers   AAV &
COMPLETE POST / Sound Editing   THUNDER TRACKS / ADR
Recording   SPECTRUM / Catering   HARLEY TO ROSE /
Completion Guarantors   FILM FINANCES / Insurance   STEEVES

LUMLEY / Laboratory   CINEVEX / Lab Liaison   IAN ANDERSON
/ Opticals   IAN SHEATH / Camera Equipment   SAMUELSONS /
Titles   OPTICAL & GRAPHIC / Title Design   DAVID / Production
Consultants   JEREMY BURKE   EMILY OLIVE   CATHY
DUNCOMBE **MUSIC CREDITS**: Original Music   JOHN
CLIFFORD WHITE / Original Song   GAVIN FRIDAY & MAURICE
SEEZER / Music Supervisor   CHRIS GOUGH / Music Supervision
MANA MUSIC / Recorded & mixed by SCOTT HEMMING / Music
Recorded at   METROPOLIS / JOHN CLIFFORD WHITE original
score recorded and mixed by SCOTT HEMMING at METROPOLIS
AUDIO, AUSTRALIA / REAL WORLD RECORDS and PETER
GABRIEL remixed by STEVEN BRAY at REAL WORLD STUDIOS,
England / "UNTIL I'M IN YOU", Composed by Gavin Friday and
Maurice Seezer, Published by Friday, Seezer Music ©1995, Performed by
Anneli M. Drecker and the Big No No, Produced by Tim Simenon,
Gavin Friday and Maurice Seezer, Recorded by Q and mixed by Tim
Simenon at RAK Studios, London / "SYGYT KHOOMEI
KARGYRAA", Traditional arranged by Boris Salchak, Published by
WOMAD Music Ltd, EMI Virgin Music Ltd, Performed by Shu-de,
©1994, Real World Records Ltd / "SPIRIT IN THE SKY", Composed by
Norman Greenbaum, Published by Essex Music Australia Pty Ltd,
Performed by Norman Greenbaum, Courtesy of Transtone Productions
/ "VERY VERY HUNGRY", Composed by Brian Eno and David
Byrne, Published by EG Music, BMG Music, Warner Chappell Music
Australia, Performed by David Byrne and Brian Eno, Courtesy of Virgin
Records / "ANGEL TECH", Composed by Richard Norris, Dave Ball,
Alex Gifford and Sheila Chandra, Published by M62, BMG Music
Publishing Co, WOMAD Music Ltd, EMI Virgin Music Ltd, Moonsung
Music, Performed by The Grid, ©1994 Real World Records Ltd / "MY
SPECIAL ANGEL", Composed by Jimmy Duncan, Published by Yale
Music Corp, J. Albert & Son, Performed by The Vogues, Courtesy of
Warner Bros Record Inc, By arrangement with Warner Special Products /
"SEA OF VAPOURS"/"TRACERY", Composed by Michael Brook,
Published by Opal Music (except North America by Opala Music Inc,
BMI, Performed by Nusrat Fateh Ali Khan, ©1990, Real World Records
Ltd / "WE DO WHAT WE'RE TOLD milgram's 37", Composed by
Peter Gabriel, Published by Real World Music Ltd, EMI Virgin Music
Ltd, Performed by Peter Gabriel, ©1986, Peter Gabriel Ltd / "ON
YOUR SHORE", Composed by Enya, Published by EMI Music
Publishing Australia Ltd, Performed by Enya, Courtesy of Warner Music
UK Ltd / "ASTRAL", Composed by Dave Clayton, Performed by Dave

Clayton and Renaud Pion, Spectral Recording, DOLBY STEREO, DIGITAL, VERIFY THEATRE FORMAT.
The Production wishes to thank CATRIONA HUGHES   OPTUS CAROMA INDUSTRIES   IMPAX COMMUNICATIONS HYLAND & SONS SECURITY DOORS   DAVID PULBROOK & PETER WHERRETT   ROSE DORITY & PHIL HEYWOOD.
The Director wishes to thank TERRY SMITH   ROZ DARBY PHILLIPA CASTLE   DR HERBERT BOWER   DR CHRISTOPHER S. AMENSON, PH.D.   PAULO REID & MEMBERS OF THE ST KILDA DROP-IN CENTRE   STAFF & MEMBERS OF ALDEN HOUSE, GLENDALE.
Developed with the assistance of Film Victoria, South Australian Film Corporation, New South Wales Film & Television Office. Script developed with the assistance of the Australian Film Commission.

SCREENPLAYS FROM CURRENCY PRESS

Strictly Ballroom
Baz Luhrmann and Craig Pearce

The Adventures of Priscilla, Queen of the Desert
Stephan Elliott

Muriel's Wedding
P.J. Hogan

The Sum of Us
David Stevens

Bad Boy Bubby
Rolf de Heer

Cosi
Louis Nowra

Dead Heart
Nick Parsons

Children of the Revolution
Peter Duncan

ALL INQUIRIES TO:
Currency Press,
PO Box 452,
Paddington,
NSW 2021
Tel: 02 9332 1300
Fax: 02 9332 3848
E-mail: currency@magna.com.au
WWW: http://www.currency.com.au